# THE KING
## OF JAM
## SANDWICHES

# THE KING OF JAM SANDWICHES

Eric Walters

ORCA BOOK PUBLISHERS

Published in Canada and the United States in 2020 by Orca Book Publishers.
orcabook.com

**Library and Archives Canada Cataloguing in Publication**
Title: The king of jam sandwiches / Eric Walters.
Names: Walters, Eric, 1957– author.
Identifiers: Canadiana (print) 20200184911 | Canadiana (ebook) 20200184920 |
ISBN 9781459825567 (softcover) | ISBN 9781459825574 (PDF) |
ISBN 9781459825581 (EPUB)
Classification: LCC PS8595.A598 K56 2020 | DDC jc813/.54—dc23

Library of Congress Control Number: 2020931816

**Summary:** Thirteen-year-old Robbie never knows from one day to the next
if there is going to be enough to eat or if his father will even come home.

Orca Book Publishers is committed to reducing the consumption
of nonrenewable resources in the making of our books. We make
every effort to use materials that support a sustainable future.

Orca Book Publishers gratefully acknowledges the support for its publishing
programs provided by the following agencies: the Government of Canada,
the Canada Council for the Arts and the Province of British Columbia
through the BC Arts Council and the Book Publishing Tax Credit.

Cover design by Rachel Page
Cover artwork by Chumphon Whangchom / EyeEm/Getty Images.

Printed and bound in Canada.

23  22  21  20  •  1  2  3  4

## ★ AUTHOR NOTE ✦

This was a difficult story for me to write because it's so personal. Many of the things I've written about are from my life. The question I'm already being asked is, How much of this is true? The answer is simple—too much and not enough.

# ONE

"Wake up!"

My eyes popped open. It was my father.

"What...what?" I mumbled.

"Get up!" he insisted.

The room was dark except for the light coming in from the hall. Outside the window there was nothing but night.

"What time is it?"

"It's time for you to get up. Get up now!" He sounded scared. Did that mean I should be scared too?

My father grabbed me by the arm and practically dragged me out of bed. I scrambled to get my feet free of my sleeping bag and onto the floor.

"You have to come downstairs…right now…now." It wasn't as much an order as a plea.

"Can't it wait until morning?"

"I'll be dead by morning!"

He let go of my arm and left the room. I heard the sound of his feet pounding down the stairs. He might not come back upstairs. Or he might come back in a few minutes. There was no way of telling. There was *never* any way of telling. I could only predict the range of possibilities. He'd said he was going to be "dead by morning." I'd heard that one before. It should have made it easier. It didn't. At least I knew what to expect. Maybe. I hoped.

I sat on the edge of my bed and took a couple of deep breaths to try to stop myself from shaking and to slow down my head and my heart. I shook my arms and flexed my wrists. I reached out one hand and grabbed the clock off the dresser. Nine minutes after three. My alarm wasn't going to go off for another three hours. I wondered if I should just go back to sleep. Maybe he'd leave me alone. But I knew that wasn't likely. I could hear him banging around downstairs. He was fully revved up. There was no way he was going to settle, and that meant I couldn't either.

Besides, what if he really *did* die tonight? What if this was the last time I would ever see him and I just rolled over and went back to sleep and then found him dead in the morning? How would I live with that? I couldn't risk it.

I stood up and padded across the floor and down the stairs, trying to avoid the steps that creaked. It was a game I always played, trying to move without being seen or heard, trying to be invisible. I walked through the living room and peeked around the corner into the kitchen. My father was pacing back and forth like a caged animal. He suddenly saw me. There was a wildness in his eyes as he looked up at me.

"I'm going to die," he said.

"Dad, you're going to be okay."

"I won't live to see morning."

"You will. I know—"

"You don't know anything!" he yelled.

The force of his words startled me, and it took me a few seconds to recover. "Dad, you didn't die the last time or the time before—"

"You sound disappointed about that," he snapped.

I knew that anything I said now would only make it worse.

His gaze fell to the floor, and his voice softened. "This time is different. I know it."

Of course, he didn't know it, but that didn't stop him from believing it. He hadn't died the first time he'd woken me up and dragged me out of bed, telling me he was certain his time was up. Or the second or the third or the times after that. And he wasn't going to die this time either.

"My heart is coming through my chest!" he exclaimed. "I'm having a heart attack! It's going to explode!"

"You're just feeling anxious, Dad," I replied. "You have to try to relax. It'll be okay." I tried to sound calm despite my own rising anxiety. Even with all the times he had done this, it was hard not to believe him.

"What do you think you are, a doctor?" he demanded.

"Of course I'm not a—"

"You're just some snot-nosed thirteen-year-old who thinks he's smarter than his father."

I took another deep breath and said nothing. I used to argue with him. I used to get angry and even yell at him. Not now. There really wasn't any point.

"So when did you get your medical degree?" he continued.

I didn't answer. I didn't say what I wanted to say.

"Where was I when that happened? I think I would have noticed you going to medical school," he said with a sneer.

I swallowed my anger. He was hardly here to notice anything. A month back I'd gone away for a few days. I'd told him I was going to be staying with a friend, and he'd never even asked what friend or how long I was going to be gone or where my friend lived or anything. I couldn't help but think that if I hadn't let him know my plans, he wouldn't have even noticed I was gone. When I came home three days later, he didn't say a word.

"Dad, I need to get to sleep. I have an important test tomorrow."

"Fine. Go back to bed then. You can just step over my body in the morning on your way to take your precious test."

His words were coming faster now. It wasn't a good sign.

"Is that test more important than your father?"

"No, it's not more important than you, Dad. I just need to get to sleep. I have school."

"And I have work."

I nearly blurted out, *Not if you're dead* but managed to keep my words in my head and my expression neutral.

"It's always about you, isn't it?" he said.

"What?"

"I'm dying, and you're worried about your little test."

I almost laughed. But laughing wouldn't get me anything except more grief.

"Are you going to be this smug and amused at my funeral?"

Obviously I hadn't hidden my thoughts or expression as well as I'd thought. My father was always good at reading people—well, everybody but himself. I had to go in another direction.

"Do you want me to call an ambulance?" I asked. I said that partly to try to calm him down and partly because I was really starting to get worried. No matter how many times he'd said this before, maybe this time it was true. Why not? People did die. I'd seen it.

"I'd rather die here in my own house. Here, where everybody else…"

He let the sentence hang. There was no need to say anything more. It wasn't like I'd forgotten who had lived here before and was no longer alive.

My father sat down at the kitchen table. I hadn't expected that. I'd thought he'd run out of the house or at least keep pacing the room.

"You need to sit down," he said.

I still didn't want to sit down, but there was no point in arguing. No point in trying to reason. No point in anything. I sat down in my regular spot at the far end of the table, facing him at the other. Ghosts occupied the three other seats.

"Why are you sitting way down there?" he asked.

"This is where I always sit."

"You can't see these from there." He tapped his finger on the table.

It was then that I saw the papers laid out in front of him. Okay, this was new. I felt the hairs on the back of my neck stand up. New was never good. I stood up and dragged my chair closer to him.

He gave me a questioning look. "Why didn't you just take the chair beside me?"

"I like this chair."

"They're all the same."

No. They weren't. This was *my* chair. The other people were gone, but those chairs were still *their* chairs. I didn't want to sit in the places of dead people.

I sat down. I focused on the papers. It was easier than looking at him. One stack was bills. I knew all about bills. Sometimes I was the one who went online to pay them.

The stack beside the bills was what looked like bank statements. My father had always been cagey about how much money we had. All I really knew was that we didn't have enough to buy much of anything.

Beside those two piles was a handwritten sheet. It was the one I was most curious about, but it was partially covered by one of the bills.

I felt something brush against my legs. It was my dog, Candy, her big eyes searching mine. I reached down and gave her a scratch behind the ear. She pressed against me. She seemed to know I needed some comfort. She was always around when I needed her.

"I have to explain all these to you so you can deal with them," said my father.

I startled back to this reality. "I know about the bills. You get me to pay them sometimes."

My father slammed his hand down hard on the papers. I jumped in my seat.

"I'm going to be dead by morning, so you're going to have to pay them *all* the time. Do you think a dead person can pay bills?"

I shook my head.

"Then stop talking and just listen while I explain it."

He picked up the first bill and went through the details. I wasn't really listening, but I tried to nod my head at the right times. Then he grabbed the next one. And the next one. He explained how much each should be and what to do if there was a problem. Then he turned to the pile of bank statements. He started with the account password.

"Say it back to me," he said.

"What?"

"Say it out loud. If you don't memorize it, you won't be able to get the money you need to pay the bills."

"Okay. It's Chambers170."

"Good."

It wasn't hard to memorize. It was our street address. Might as well have been *password* or *123456*. If I were in charge, I'd change it to something less easy to hack. Maybe a few days from now, when he had calmed down again, I'd talk to him about changing it.

But for now all I could think about was how strange it was that we were even having this conversation. He'd never talked about our bank account before, never told me how to get into it. Was he really going to die?

As far as the account went, I was more than surprised—I was shocked. Turned out we had much more money than I thought we had. Not a fortune but enough that we could have afforded more things. Things like food. We didn't have to be eating only potatoes and apples and bread and jam. I *hated* jam sandwiches.

There were six envelopes on the table. I knew each one probably contained money. There was always cash stashed away in envelopes around the house. My father didn't completely trust the banks, and he liked to have money handy "just in case." He pulled the money out of each envelope, counted it out for me and then put the money back. The amount in each varied but as he counted, I did the math in my head. A total of $585. Good. And now I could access the money in the bank too if I needed it. And if he died, I was sure I'd need it.

"Now there's one final thing," my father said. He picked up the handwritten sheet and put it right in front of me.

"These are the arrangements for my funeral."

My father had always been convinced he was dying of cancer or suffering from some mysterious disease that hadn't been diagnosed because doctors were all "a bunch of bloodsucking idiots." But this was the first time he'd talked about his funeral with me. The thought popped into my head again that maybe this time it *was* different—maybe he *was* dying.

He tapped his finger on the paper. "This is important. Don't waste money on flowers, and don't let them convince you to buy some fancy casket."

I felt numb. My best defense had always been to be prepared, to anticipate what he'd say or do next, but I hadn't seen this one coming.

"Of course, because you're only thirteen it'll be your uncle Jack making the arrangements, but I need you to make sure he doesn't waste my money."

Uncle Jack was my father's brother. He was a nice man who liked to tell silly jokes. He seemed to get along with everybody. Everybody except my father.

"You have to be there to speak for me because I won't be able to speak for myself. I worked hard for every dollar I ever got, and Jack just throws money around."

He went on and on, telling me about the people he wanted invited to the funeral and the people he wanted barred at the door. What did he want me to do? Stand there and tell them they couldn't come in? He listed a couple of hymns he wanted sung, though we never went to church. He'd told me he stopped believing in God the day my mother died. I didn't remember her dying—or living. I was too young then.

My grandfather and grandmother had lived with us. My grandfather died a year after my mother, and my grandmother six months after him. I had fuzzy memories of my grandfather, but I remembered my grandmother and her funeral clearly.

I looked at the other chairs around the table. In a very short time we had gone from a full house to just my father and me. He was the only one who had lived, and he was the one who kept threatening to die.

"Do you have any questions?" he asked.

I shook my head. I didn't. None that I was stupid enough to ask, that is. Oh. I'd thought of one.

"What happens to me?"

"The money that's left, assuming you don't let your uncle Jack waste it all on a funeral, will be left to you in trust. You'll get it when you're eighteen."

"I meant now, after you're…you're gone."

"The system will take care of you."

"The system? What does that mean?" I asked.

"Foster care. You'll go into a foster home. Those people will take care of you. They get paid to— it's a job. I'm sure most of them might be okay people, but I've heard some pretty terrible stories… you know, in the newspapers and on TV."

"But what about Uncle Jack and Aunt Cora? Couldn't I live with them?"

He laughed. "What makes you think they'd want to take you in?"

I felt my heart sink.

"Their children are all grown. Do you think they're crazy enough to want to go back to taking care of a kid again, to taking care of *you*?"

I didn't answer. There *was* no answer.

"If they cared for you that much, they'd come around more often," he said.

He was right. They didn't come around a lot. They had when I was little, but every time they came a fight would break out between my father and my uncle. I used to spend a few weeks every summer at their cottage. That had stopped a couple of years ago.

"When was the last time they dropped in to see us?" he asked.

"I don't know," I said. I did. It was over three months ago, and they'd left when my father got into the usual big fight with my uncle.

"Any more questions?" he asked.

I shook my head.

"Good. Now you can go to bed…if you want."

I got to my feet. My legs were shaking as I walked out of the room. I didn't look back. He had told me everything he wanted to tell me. I was set. I could handle whatever happened.

But he wasn't really going to die tonight. Probably not. And even if he did, I had at least talked to him.

I'd never gotten that chance with my mother, as far as I knew. Sometimes I wondered what I would have said to her if I had known she was going to die. Sometimes I still talked to her in my head. Actually, not sometimes. A lot. Maybe that was strange, talking to a person I couldn't even remember talking to when she was alive. But it made me feel better.

I climbed the stairs and got into bed. I crawled back into my sleeping bag, pulled the zipper up and pushed my head down, so I was almost completely covered. I held my breath and listened. I was hoping he'd played himself out, that by going downstairs I had calmed him enough that he'd let me sleep for what was left of the night.

I heard Candy's toenails clicking up the stairs. She padded into my bedroom and jumped onto my bed. I opened the zipper of my sleeping bag, and she climbed in beside me. She was warm and soft, and even with her stinky dog breath, it felt good when she started to lick my face.

"Don't worry, girl. It'll be okay." I said that to her a lot. "No matter what happens, I'll take care of you. I promise."

I knew my father would likely be alive in the morning. Sometimes I thought that maybe, just maybe, it would be better if he did die. Then I could stop anticipating the worst and get on with it. Waiting was hard, but it was all part of the plan. One more day down. One more day closer.

# TWO

The next morning when my eyes popped open, I didn't know what was happening for a split second. I had kicked off my sleeping bag, and Candy was gone. I'd managed to go back to sleep, but what time was it now? It was light, and I could read the clock. Six twenty-five. The alarm was set for six thirty, but I always seemed to wake up just before the alarm.

As I climbed out of bed, the memories of the previous night all flooded back. It was like a dream. Actually, more like a nightmare. Or one of those movies where they keep killing the monster and it keeps coming back to life. Except this monster hadn't died—it had only threatened to die.

I stopped moving and listened. There were no sounds. Nothing. My father had probably left for work. His job was on the far side of the city, and he had to be out early to beat the traffic. He was already gone. Or dead. Or dead. Or dead. Or dead. It was like an echo in my head. What if I walked downstairs and found him slumped over the table or lying on the floor? I couldn't let myself think like that. He had gone to work. Simple as that. But I wouldn't know for sure until I went downstairs. I didn't want to do it alone.

I whistled, and almost instantly I heard Candy's toenails tapping along the floor and racing up the stairs. She jumped against me, practically knocking me backward and off my feet.

I walked over to my dresser, pulled out the bottom drawer and rearranged the clothing so I could pull out the notebook. A pen clipped in the middle opened it to the right place. Taking the pen, I crossed out *1,627* and wrote *1,626* instead. I closed the notebook and hid it away again.

I walked down the hall, Candy at my heels, and hesitated before looking into my father's room.

He wasn't in there. No body. The bed hadn't been slept in. That meant he had slept on the couch. He did that a lot. Or maybe it meant he was downstairs. Dead.

"Don't be stupid," I muttered under my breath.

I went down the stairs but stopped before entering the kitchen. What would I do if he *was* dead? Would I just go to school and take my test and act like nothing was wrong? I was pretty good at pretending nothing was wrong.

There was something I could do before I looked into the kitchen. I spun around, went to the front window and looked outside. The car wasn't in the driveway. My father had gone to work. He wasn't dead. Not today, at least.

Life was going to go on, and there was so much I had to do before I could leave for school. I ran back upstairs with Candy barking and nipping at my heels. For her this was a game. I peeled off my pajama top, threw some water on my face and then, using a little sliver of soap and a facecloth that wasn't much more than a rag, I washed my pits.

Back in my room I looked through the pile of clothes on the floor waiting to be washed. It wasn't like I had many clothes, but it had been a while since I'd done any laundry because we were out of detergent.

My pants were clean enough, so there was no problem there. I picked up a shirt and did the smell test. It didn't pass inspection. I tossed it into the corner and grabbed another one. Before I even smelled it, I noticed a red stain. Spaghetti sauce. I tossed that shirt over with the first one and picked up a third. This one passed both tests.

There wasn't time to walk Candy, eat breakfast, study a bit more, pack my lunch and get to school without being late. I put her out in the backyard. She deserved better, but I'd make it up to her later.

* ★ *

The aroma of the pizza wafting through the air signaled it was almost lunchtime. On pizza days everyone seemed a little more excited than usual.

Of course, I just had my usual crappy jam sandwich. I didn't have any extra money to buy pizza.

The bell finally rang, and people jumped up and rushed for the door. I grabbed my stuff too.

"Robbie, can you wait a second?" asked Mr. Yeoman. He was my homeroom and language arts teacher.

"Um, sure." I felt anxious. I had the stupidest thought, that he was going to tell me I'd done badly on the test we'd taken, but he wouldn't have marked it yet, and besides, I knew I'd done well. I always did well.

Sal, my best friend since second grade, stopped beside my desk and leaned in close. "Don't worry," he said.

"I'm not worried."

"Sure you're not. He probably wants to tell you why you're his favorite student. See you in the caf."

Sal and I ate lunch together every day. It was Sal, me, Taylor, Raj and Jay. That was my pack, and we'd eaten together almost every day from seventh grade on. We always sat in the same place in the cafeteria, and we talked about movies and superheroes and school and sports.

"And, Harmony, can you stay as well?" Mr. Yeoman called out.

Harmony was new—this was her first day. I looked at her, and she scowled at me. As the last couple of stragglers left the room, I waited beside Mr. Yeoman's desk. He and I both waited as Harmony slowly gathered her stuff and then, even more slowly, made her way up to the front.

"Harmony," Mr. Yeoman began, "this is a big school, and it can take some getting used to. So, Robbie, I want you to show her around, help her settle in."

"Him?" The look on Harmony's face had changed from complete disdain to complete disgust.

"Me?" What was Mr. Yeoman thinking? This was not a good idea at all.

"Yes, you, Robbie. You can be Harmony's guide for the next day or so." He turned to Harmony. "He's very responsible. Very mature."

She snorted.

"It's time for lunch, so Robbie will show you where the cafeteria is. I'm sure he'll even let you sit at his table, won't you, Robbie?"

"Sure…if she wants."

Harmony's expression made it clear she most certainly did not want to do that. I wasn't so thrilled with it either, and I didn't know how the guys would feel about it.

"I started a new school when I was about your age, and I remember how tough it was, so I thought you could use a little help," Mr. Yeoman explained.

"I don't need any help," Harmony said.

"Everybody needs help. Now off you go. Robbie, you're in charge. Understand?"

"Sure."

"Good. Now go get some lunch."

I left the room first. Harmony was a few steps behind me. When she stepped out into the hall, she made a hard turn to the right.

"Wait, the cafeteria is this way!"

She kept walking. I looked back through the open classroom door, hoping Mr. Yeoman hadn't heard.

"Go get her!" he called.

Great. She had already turned a corner and gone out of sight. I ran after her.

"Wait!"

She stopped, turned and scowled. Was that her only expression?

"The cafeteria is the other way."

"I don't care."

"But I'm supposed to take you to the cafeteria."

"You're not taking me anywhere," she snapped.

"But Mr. Yeoman told me to—"

"Screw him and screw you."

I felt a rush of anger and almost yelled, *Screw you too*. But I knew that wouldn't help. I took a deep breath.

"Look, I know a school this big, with this many people, can be scary."

"Do I look scared?"

She didn't look scared. She looked *scary*. But it occurred to me that maybe she was so nervous she was trying extra hard not to look scared. Like when people laugh when they really want to cry.

"You can come to my table and sit with me and my friends."

"You have friends?" she asked.

"What?" *Did she really just say what I think she said?*

"I was just surprised that you have friends. I thought he wanted me to sit with you so you wouldn't have to sit by yourself anymore."

"I've got lots of friends," I replied, puffing up a bit. Okay, maybe not *lots*, but really, who had more than a few?

"I just thought your mummy was your best friend."

"What?" What a jerk! Why was I wasting my time with this girl? If she didn't want to come with me, well, who cared?

"It's just that it looks like your mummy dresses you…and probably in the dark."

I felt the pit of my stomach tighten and anger starting to form. I couldn't let that happen. I took another deep breath to calm myself.

But when she turned and started to walk away, I reached out and grabbed her arm. Quick as lightning, she brushed off my arm, spun around and glared at me. "Don't you *ever* touch me again," she said, eyes blazing.

I was shocked. I hadn't meant to grab her. I had just reacted.

"If you ever touch me again, I'll pop you in the nose."

"You're going to *pop* me in the nose?" I said with a nervous laugh. "What is this, a cartoon?"

"Go away and leave me alone or I'm going to smack you."

"Look, I don't like this any more than you do. I'm just trying to—"

Her fist smashed into my nose, and pain shot up into my skull. I staggered backward and screamed.

"What did you do?" I yelled through my hands, which were clutching my nose—my bleeding nose. I felt my eyes tearing up.

"I did what I told you I was going to do."

"Are you crazy?" I blinked back the tears. Bleeding was bad enough. I didn't need to add tears.

"Do you want another?" she asked.

I took a slight step back and held out one bloody hand to try to protect myself. If she tried to hit me again, I'd show her exactly what—

"What is going on here?" a deep voice asked.

I spun around. It was Mr. Arseneau, the school principal.

"Your nose! What happened?" he demanded. He sounded angry, but he looked concerned.

"Were you two fighting?" he asked.

"No, sir. I don't do that…not anymore."

"Did she hit you?"

I looked back at Harmony. Now she did look scared.

I wanted to swear at her. I wanted to hit her— at least, I wanted to tell the principal what had happened. I wasn't going to do any of those things.

"No, sir, of course not, sir…I just fell…tripped on my feet and smashed into the locker." I pointed at the row of lockers like somehow they would verify my story.

His expression changed to disbelief. "Really? Is that what happened?"

"Yes, sir. Ask Harmony."

Harmony hesitated for a second before replying. "I didn't see him fall against anything."

What was she doing? Was she trying to get us suspended?

"But I heard a big smash," she continued. "Like somebody had kicked the locker. I turned around and saw him picking himself up off the floor."

Wow, she described it so convincingly I could almost picture it happening.

"And I feel bad because it was all my fault," she continued.

Yeah, of course it was. But why tell a lie and then follow it up with the truth?

"Robert was acting as my guide," said Harmony.

Robert? Nobody ever called me Robert.

"Mr. Yeoman sent Robert after me. He saw that I got turned around, and Robert was coming after me to bring me to the cafeteria and he was running, and that's when he fell and that's why it's my fault. If I'd have known where I was going in the first place, this whole thing wouldn't have happened."

"Yes, sir, that's exactly what happened," I said.

Mr. Arseneau looked like he didn't believe our story. I gave him a bit more.

"If she *had* punched me, I would want her to be suspended."

"And I wouldn't have any choice. You certainly know the rules about that."

"Yes, I do."

"Let's take a look at that nose," he said.

As I took my hand away, some blood dripped onto the floor. Mr. Arseneau carefully put two fingers on the bridge of my nose and gave it a little wiggle.

"Does that hurt?"

"Not really."

"That's good. I don't think it's broken, but you should go to the office and get some ice on it to keep down the swelling."

"Yes, sir."

"And you should go with him," he said to Harmony.

"Me?" she asked.

"It's Harmony, right?"

"Yeah."

"You must be new."

"She started today," I said.

"Welcome to Osler Middle School. I'll assure you we're not usually this exciting."

"I don't mind a little excitement," she said.

Not only did she not mind excitement, but she clearly wasn't opposed to causing it either.

# THREE

Mr. Arseneau got a call on his radio—he was needed someplace else. He told us again to go to the office and then rushed off.

"You don't have to go with me," I said.

"I have nowhere else I have to be."

"It's this way."

I noticed I was still leaving a little trail of blood droplets behind me. A few kids stared as we passed. Thankfully, none were people I really knew. And I was even more grateful that nobody had seen what had really happened.

"Why didn't you tell him that I punched you?" Harmony asked.

"I'm no rat. I didn't want to get you suspended."

"Would he really have suspended me?"

"School policy. You fight, you get suspended. First offense, one day. Second, three days, and the third is a full week."

"I'll keep that in mind if I ever want a few days off," she said. "Why do you even care if I'm suspended?"

"According to Mr. Yeoman, I'm supposed to take care of you…at least for a few days."

She laughed. "I can take care of myself. Probably better than you can." She paused. "But you certainly can take a punch."

"Gee, thanks…although instead of insulting me, maybe you should be thanking me for not turning you in."

"Maybe you should think more about not annoying me so I don't have to punch you again."

More kids stared as we passed them.

"And maybe you should keep your voice down so somebody else doesn't tell the office what really happened and you *do* get suspended for fighting."

"Fighting? That would involve you trying to hit me back instead of just bleeding all over everything."

I wanted to tell her that if she ever did this again, she'd get the fight she wanted so bad. But instead I said, "How about we just shut up about this and never tell anybody what really happened."

"Sure. We could shake on it, but I don't want your blood on me."

I was still dripping. Some of it was on my shirt and some was on my pants and there were even a few specks on my left shoe.

"Here we are," I said as we got to the office. There were a couple of kids sitting in chairs, and I was relieved I didn't recognize either of them.

"Actually, if you think about it, you *are* showing me around the school," Harmony said. "Knowing where the office is will probably come in handy."

We walked up to the counter.

"Oh my goodness!" said Mrs. Henry, the head secretary, when she saw my face. "Robbie, what happened?"

"I tripped. Mr. Arseneau sent me here to get cleaned up and get some ice."

"And you?" she asked Harmony.

"I was told to bring Robert here."

"Wait...aren't you the one who just started here today?"

"Yeah," said Harmony.

"Would you mind going and getting me some wet paper towels?" asked Mrs. Henry.

"Me?" Harmony asked.

"Yes. The washroom is just off to the left. Thanks, hon."

I expected Harmony to refuse or say something sarcastic. Instead she turned and walked away, heading for the washroom. Mrs. Henry opened the office fridge, pulled out a little plastic bag filled with ice and handed it to me.

"Sit," she ordered.

I took one of the remaining seats, and she knelt down beside me.

"Hold it right there," she said, pressing the bag to my face.

The bag was cold and felt good.

She turned to the two students sitting beside me. "You two go grab lunch and then come back closer to the bell."

They didn't need to be told twice. They got up and raced down the hall.

"So you tripped, did you?" she asked me.

"Yes."

"And you couldn't get your hands up in time?"

"I tried, but I'm clumsy. My father says I'm still growing into my feet."

"And you're *sure* you weren't in a fight?" she asked.

"Positive."

Harmony reappeared with a mass of sopping paper towels. She handed them all to me. Water dripped onto my pants as I started to try to wipe away the blood.

The office phone started ringing. Mrs. Henry stood up and said, "Okay, it looks like the bleeding is slowing down. But you should stay put until it stops completely."

She retreated to the other side of the counter to answer the ringing phone. Harmony sat down in the chair beside me.

"Hand me a couple of those," she said. She took a couple of the paper towels from me and began patting my face. It was tender when she touched close to my nose.

"Thanks," I said.

"I guess I should be the one thanking you, Robert."

"Everybody calls me Robbie."

"Do you think I *care* even a little what everybody else calls you?"

"Probably not."

"Besides, you're much more a Robert than a Robbie," she said.

"And what exactly does that mean?"

"Robbie is sort of a cartoony, friendly creature who smiles all the time. Maybe the name of the mascot for the Olympics or something. That's not you."

"Thanks, I think."

"Mascots always wander around smiling at people. That's not you. You, you're not the smiling sort. You're the serious kind, the always-trying-to-figure-things-out kind."

I shrugged. She wasn't wrong, but how did she know all of this?

"I saw you watching people in class. I do that too," she said before I could ask. "It's important to pay attention. You never know where danger is going to come from."

"That was definitely proved today."

She laughed. "You're funny too. And smart."

"I guess we'll have to wait to see how I did on the test today."

"Don't you usually do well?"

I nodded. "Top of the class…even though I'm the youngest."

"December birthday?"

"March, but a year after everybody else. I skipped a grade."

"Then your being called Robert makes even more sense. More serious. Studious."

"If we're changing names, then maybe I shouldn't call you Harmony," I suggested.

"What *should* my name be?"

I pretended to think for a second. "Hmm. Well, from what I've seen so far, maybe *Disharmony* would suit you better."

She laughed again. "You really are funny."

"I hope you mean funny hilarious, not funny-looking."

"It could be both. But let's go with semi-hilarious."

"I'll take semi."

She continued gently dabbing the wet paper towels on my face. It was a bit strange to be this close to her, especially since she was staring so intently at me. It almost felt like she was trying to look *inside* me. I wanted to move or turn away or get away completely, but I couldn't. Besides, the wet paper towel felt good against my nose.

"Do you get in a lot of fights?" she asked.

"Why would you think that?"

"The way the principal grilled you and the secretary looked at you. I just thought it had happened before. You know."

"It's just that they were worried about me. People worry, you know."

"Not that I've seen. People don't worry as much as they give you reasons to be worried."

I wanted to tell her I understood what she was saying. But how could I say that to a stranger, especially one who'd just punched me?

"There. You're all cleaned up, and the bleeding has stopped, I think," she said.

She took the red-stained wad of paper towels and threw it into the garbage can. It landed with a thud.

I was feeling strangely shy and didn't know what to say or do next.

"It seems only fair that I should clean up what I caused," she whispered.

"Yeah." I smiled and then stood up and dropped the ice bag into the garbage can as well.

Mrs. Henry looked up at the sound. "You okay now? There's still twenty minutes before lunch is over," she said. "You should try to grab something to eat."

"We will."

As we stepped out of the office, I said, "Senior lockers are this way. Let's grab our lunches. I can finally show you to the cafeteria."

When we got to my locker, I angled my body to block her view as I dialed in the combination numbers. The lock clicked. I removed it and opened the locker door.

"Wow, that's impressive. Or a little scary," she said.

"What do you mean?"

"I've never seen a locker so organized."

"I just like to know where everything is. Is there something wrong with that?"

"No, I guess not. It's just that the only person I know who was that organized is my uncle Joey. And he's in the federal penitentiary now."

"I'm not going to go to jail. I'm going to university."

"You sound pretty sure about that," she said.

"I am. I get good marks, and I haven't had a single detention for more than a year," I said—and almost instantly regretted it.

"Strange. I've known you for less than a day, and already you've been in a fight and lied to the principal."

"I thought we both agreed that my getting punched didn't really qualify as a fight."

She laughed. I felt confused. Was she laughing at my joke or at me?

I put all my morning-class books away in their spots and pulled out my lunch and what I'd need for my afternoon classes.

"So why *didn't* it turn into a fight?" Harmony asked.

"You mean why didn't I punch you back?"

She nodded.

"I didn't want to get suspended."

Part of me wanted to tell her I hadn't had a fight in close to two years. But I was worried she would make fun of me for *not* fighting. I guess I could have told her how many fights I'd been in before that if I wanted to impress her in a different way.

I closed the locker and snapped the lock back in place. "Where's your locker so we can grab your lunch?" I asked.

She didn't answer, and she also didn't move.

"Look, it's no big deal. Let's get your lunch and head to the cafeteria. Don't make me force you into punching me again."

She laughed and shook her head, and we started walking.

"Look, I don't have a lunch, so we don't have to go to my locker. Besides, I really don't want to go to the cafeteria," she said.

"How about I share my lunch with you?"

"It depends on what you've got," she said.

"Does it matter?"

"I guess not, but could we still just eat somewhere else?"

"Why not the cafeteria?"

"It's just hard, you know, to walk into a new place and not know where to sit and feel like everybody is staring at you."

"Which is exactly why Mr. Yeoman wanted me to take you there to begin with."

She gave me a sideways glance that clearly told me to shut up.

My nose and I decided to listen to her wordless warning.

"Where do you want to eat instead?" I asked.

"Here is good."

"The hall?"

"Why not? It's quiet, and there's nobody to bug me other than you."

Harmony hoisted herself onto the ledge of a window. I threw up my pack and sat down on the other side of it. I pulled out an apple, a banana and the zip-lock bag that held the jam sandwich.

"Is that it?" Harmony asked.

"I was rushed this morning and didn't have time to pack anything else."

"Your mother doesn't pack your lunch?"

I could have told her that I didn't have a mother—that she'd been dead so long I didn't even really know her. But I didn't. That was none of Harmony's business.

"I like to take care of myself," I explained.

"Doesn't look like you're doing such a great job," Harmony said.

"What does that mean?"

"You're *so* skinny."

"I'm thin, not skinny."

"No, you're so skinny that I feel guilty eating part of your lunch—is that *jam*?"

"Strawberry."

"If it's going to be jam, it has to be strawberry. That's my favorite," she said.

I opened up the bag and handed her half of the sandwich.

She took a bite. "This is good."

"Yeah, I'm planning on being a chef when I grow up."

"You are?"

"Yeah, my restaurant will feature jam sandwiches, toast and boiled potatoes."

"I'd eat there."

She downed her half of the sandwich before I had even taken a second bite of mine.

"Apple or banana?" I asked.

"Which do you want?"

"I like them both. You choose."

She took the banana, and again it disappeared in a few bites.

"I know you don't want really want to be a chef," she said.

"How do you know that?"

"Because you said you want to go to university."

"Yeah, I do."

"That is so strange. What person in eighth grade talks about going to university?" she asked.

"Everybody needs a plan."

"But university? Where'd that idea come from?"

I shrugged. "Education is the way to become somebody."

"Do you even know anybody who went to university?"

I shook my head. My father hadn't graduated from high school.

"From what I've seen so far," said Harmony, "I figure this neighborhood produces people more likely to do time in jail than in university."

That was impossible to argue, because it was the truth. Lots of the older brothers and fathers of kids I knew were either in jail or had spent time there. Regardless of what he did or didn't do, my father had never gotten himself arrested.

"Not that the neighborhood I'm from is any better," she added. "And at least you have a plan."

"Don't you have a plan?"

"Sure. My plan is to get out of the foster home."

"You're in a foster home?"

"Don't sound so shocked."

"It's just that I've never known anybody in foster care. Don't worry—I won't tell anybody."

"I don't care if you tell *everybody*. It's not like it's *my* fault I'm there." She stopped and stared at me. "Besides, I get the feeling you're not somebody who blabs things. You're probably great at keeping secrets."

I was. Especially my own.

"You know, I didn't really forget my lunch today. I refused to take one, just like I refused to eat breakfast this morning."

"Why would you do that?"

"I'm not going to let them bribe me with pancakes and bacon and a roast-beef sandwich."

I tried to remember the last time I'd had any of those things. I pushed the apple toward her.

"You don't have to do that," she said.

"I had breakfast. You must be starving."

I thought she was going to argue, but she took the apple and immediately took a big bite out of it.

"So how long will this hunger strike go on?" I asked.

"It depends on what they're having for supper —unless you're having something better at your place and you're inviting me."

I laughed. "The odds are, whatever they're serving is better."

"Are you saying your mother isn't much of a cook?" she asked.

Once again she'd mentioned my mother. Had she heard something? No, probably not. She hadn't had time to talk to anybody, and it wasn't like many people knew to begin with. I never talked about not having a mother, and I wasn't exactly a subject of interest around the school.

"I won't even have time to eat a real supper tonight," I said. "I'll have to grab something fast before I go to work."

"You have a job?"

"I work at the butcher shop. I sweep the floors and clean the display cases and deliver groceries. It's just a couple of days a week after school and on Saturdays."

"How much do they pay you?"

"Enough. I'm not doing it for fun."

"Then I'm confused. You have some bucks of your own, but it's not like you're spending money on clothes. Look at you."

I was surprised how much her comment hurt my feelings. Why should I care what some random girl thought about what I wore?

"You have a strange way of saying thank you," I said.

"Look, I'm just trying to keep it real. You have to know your pants are way too short."

"They're just what I threw on this morning as I was rushing out. I don't pay attention to things like that."

"You *should* start paying attention."

I had noticed. I knew. I paid attention to everything.

"Has anyone ever told you that you're a bit insensitive?" I asked.

"Everybody, all the time. Apparently I can be a real jerk sometimes."

"That's hard to argue with," I said, nodding. "You know, you could change."

"And you could change your pants," she snapped. "That would be a lot easier."

Before I could respond—if I could have thought of something to say—the bell rang. Lunch was over.

I got up. "We better get to class."

"Wait!"

I stopped, and she came up close, practically putting her face in mine. She put a hand on my chin and moved my head slightly from side to side as she stared at me. What was she—

"Nobody will notice," she said.

"Notice what?"

"Your nose. The ice did its job. It's not really swollen."

She released her grip, turned and walked away. I stood there, stunned, for a few seconds before I ran to catch up.

# FOUR

"Hey, Robert!"

I recognized the voice and the name. I turned around.

Harmony was running toward me. "It looks like you're going in my direction."

"Oh yeah? Where do you live?"

"On Silverthorn. You're going that way, right?"

I nodded.

"Then I'll walk with you."

*Great.* I'd done what Mr. Yeoman had asked, shown the new kid around. But this was above and beyond. I'd only known Harmony for half a day and already I knew she was trouble. All afternoon I'd watched her in class without letting her know I was watching her. It wasn't anything she'd said, but I'd seen how she sneered or scoffed when people were talking. I was thankful nobody had noticed my nose.

"Where do you live?" she asked.

"Chambers—170 Chambers. That's only two streets over from Silverthorn."

"Then can you walk me right home?"

I wanted to say no, but I couldn't. "No problem. It's on the way, more or less."

We walked in silence. I thought about my pants being too short and my shirt being bloodstained. It wasn't that bad—nobody had noticed. My stomach growled. Maybe I'd make myself an extra jam sandwich to eat on the way to work.

"Looks like you didn't have to worry about that test," Harmony said finally.

Mr. Yeoman had marked them during lunch hour and handed them back. He always announced who had the highest mark. Part of me liked that, and part of me didn't. I usually tried to fly under the radar as much as possible, though everybody knew I was really smart. But sometimes being younger than

the others and getting top marks was a bad combination. I'd learned that the hard way more than once.

"I did all right."

"*All right*? You got the top mark in the class."

"Not perfect though. I missed a couple." Saying
things like this was what sometimes got me in trouble.

"Close enough. My mother would assume I'd
cheated if I ever brought home a mark like that."

I had a pretty good idea what my father's reaction
would be. I didn't want to talk about it. But there was
something I *did* want to talk about. "Can I ask you a
question?"

"You can ask me anything," said Harmony. "But
that doesn't mean I'm going to answer."

I hesitated. I'd been thinking about something
all afternoon. It had just seemed like such a coin-
cidence, meeting her after what my father had said
the night before.

"What's it like living in a foster home?" I asked.
This was safer than asking her why she was in foster
care. Besides, I wanted to know about it for me, not
for her.

"Some are okay."

"Some? You've been in more than one?"

"If you include what they call receiving homes, then more like a dozen. Some are good and some are, well, terrible."

"And this one, the one you're in now, what's it like?"

"Too early to tell. So far the food certainly *smells* good."

"You might want to try eating it and find out," I suggested. "What are the foster parents like?"

"Why are you so interested?"

I wasn't about to say *because my father threatened me with one last night.* "I'm just curious, that's all," I replied. "It's like I said, I've never known anybody who was in a foster home."

"Glad I can expand your world. Some of the foster homes are kind of creepy—you know, peeling paint and even cockroaches."

"That's awful!"

"But mostly they're just regular houses with regular people."

"And are there other foster kids with you at these places?"

"It's different at every place. At this one I'm the only foster kid there. I like that. I like having my own space. How about you? Do you have your own room?" Harmony asked.

"Yeah, I do. I don't have brothers or sisters." But talking about me was too personal and wasn't helping me get answers. "Foster parents—they get paid to take in these kids, right?"

"Sure, but I don't think it's a lot of money." She stopped walking. "This is it. Here we are."

"*This* is the foster home?" I asked. It was just a regular house.

"What were you expecting? A big sign out front? A run-down shack with broken windows?"

"No, uh…I wasn't expecting anything. Sorry." Now I was the one being a jerk. "Okay, see you at school tomorrow."

"If I haven't run away," she said.

"Maybe you should start with supper, and if it's good, then you can stick around for at least another day."

She looked surprised by what I'd said. My advice surprised me too. Why did I even care?

"I guess I'll add that to my plan," said Harmony. "See you tomorrow, Robert."

"And I'll see you tomorrow…Disharmony."

She headed up the walk. Something about this girl was different. I didn't usually like different. I liked everything safe and calm and the same as always. Harmony was none of those things.

# FIVE

I gave Candy one last scratch behind the ear and then closed the door behind me. I took three steps across the porch, turned and went back to make sure the door was locked. It was. It was always locked, but I couldn't stop myself from checking. I always checked.

I had five minutes to get to the butcher shop, and it was a ten-minute walk. I started jogging.

Walking Harmony to her place had made the trip home longer than usual, so I was short on time. Before leaving for work I'd walked Candy, peeled potatoes and put them in a pot of water on the stove, eaten another jam sandwich and changed into my work uniform. Funny, it was about the best outfit I owned, and the pants were the right length.

I took a shortcut through the alley, looking around anxiously. In this neighborhood it was always better to stay someplace more public. Alleys could be trouble. I'd have to chance it. There were big bins behind each store, overflowing with garbage. Collection day was tomorrow. It should have stunk, but the wind was blowing just right so that the smells coming from the bakery that backed onto the alley overpowered everything else. I loved the bakery. It always had great deals on day-old bread and donuts.

I hurried in through the back door of the butcher shop. I could hear Mr. and Mrs. Priamo up front serving customers. I started to break down empty cardboard boxes to go into the recycling bin. Keeping the back room and storage room clean and organized was one of my jobs. I stomped on another box, and it collapsed with a loud crash.

"Good afternoon, Robbie!" Mrs. Priamo sang out as she came into the back room.

"Good afternoon, Mrs. Priamo."

My boss was always friendly and kind to me. It made me uneasy.

"Did you get a chance to eat anything after school?" she asked.

"Yes, I grabbed something, thanks."

"It wasn't enough! You're so skinny, just skin and bones!"

I liked to think of myself as slender, but *skinny* seemed to be the word going around today. Almost involuntarily I looked down at my wrists. Maybe people were right.

"Oh, honey, I didn't mean to embarrass you," she said. "It's just that boys your age grow so fast. You need to keep feeding the furnace. Come here and sit down," she said, patting the chair by the desk.

I hesitated for a second. I really did have work to do, but it was sort of an order from my boss, wasn't it?

"I think you might like this." She took the lid off a glass container on the desk. A wonderful smell wafted out. The food inside was steaming hot.

"I made this last night and just warmed it up in the microwave. Do you like chicken parmesan?"

I shook my head. "I've never had it before."

"No? You'll love it!" she said as she handed me a knife and fork.

I cut off a little piece. The cheese was sticky and stretched out in a string as I lifted the first piece of chicken. I put it in my mouth. It was amazing.

"Do you like it?" she asked.

I shook my head. "I don't like it"—disappointment flashed across her face before I could finish my sentence—"I *love* it."

She leaned down and gave me a hug. I immediately felt anxious and uncomfortable.

"Eat, eat," she said as she released me.

I popped a second piece into my mouth. It was as good—no, even better—than the first.

I heard the bell ring over the front door. A customer coming or going. Mr. Priamo appeared in the doorway.

"Are we paying the boy to work or to eat?" he asked.

I started to get up, but Mrs. Priamo put a hand on my shoulder.

"You can't expect a car to drive unless there's fuel in the tank."

"I'm not putting fuel in somebody else's tank," said Mr. Priamo. "He can eat at home. He comes here to work."

"This boy is a worker. You know that. You've said he's the best help you've ever had!"

He said something to her in Italian, arms flying. She fired a rapid string of Italian right back at him. He tried to shush her. Her eyes flashed. A couple of times he tried to get in a word, but she wasn't going to be stopped. Finally he held up his arms in surrender.

"Eat your parm and then you get to work, okay?" he said.

"Yes, sir. I'll stay later if I need to."

"You'll leave on time. In a butcher shop, the work can never be finished."

"Thank you, sir."

"And isn't there something else you want to say?" Mrs. Priamo asked her husband.

He mumbled something under his breath in Italian and then turned to me. "Robbie, next month you will have been with us six months. So I'm going to give you a raise—not too much, but something."

"Thank you, sir!"

"Or maybe we should give you extra food instead."

"We will feed him as well," said Mrs. Priamo. "He's so skinny!"

"You think everybody is too skinny!" said Mr. Priamo.

"Not everybody!" she said, poking a finger into his belly.

They started arguing, and then Mr. Priamo wrapped his arms around his wife, picked her up and swung her around. She started giggling. I felt almost embarrassed watching them, but it made me smile.

The bell over the door tinkled. Mr. Priamo put his wife down and hurried back to the front of the store.

"No rushing," Mrs. Priamo said to me. "You eat…I have another piece. Maybe you take it home and have it for lunch tomorrow?"

I felt happy and uneasy all at once. Mrs. Priamo went out front, leaving me and the chicken alone. I finished it up quickly and got back to work.

The car was in the driveway. I wasn't surprised, but I still felt relieved, especially after the previous night. There was a light on upstairs as well as blue TV light shining out the living room window. I went inside as quietly as possible. Candy came running up, happy to see me. She was always happy to see me, although tonight the foil-wrapped chicken parm I was carrying might have been an even bigger draw. I was sure she could smell it.

I tiptoed into the living room. My father was in his chair, watching TV, although the volume was so low I could barely hear it. His head was tilted off to the side, his eyes were closed, and he was whistling through his nose. He often fell asleep in front of the TV but not usually this early. The night before must have really taken it out of him.

Candy let out a little yip, and my father's eyes popped open. He looked around, still half asleep.

"What time is it?" he mumbled.

"Twenty after nine."

"I just sat down for a minute when I got home...I must have fallen asleep...did you say it was after nine?"

"Yes, I just got home from work. Did you have a chance to do the laundry?"

"I'm barely hanging in here, and you want to know if I did the laundry?" he asked.

There was no point in saying anything more about that. "Did you eat?" I asked.

He shook his head. "I wasn't hungry. Just exhausted."

"Are you hungry now?"

"I could eat something." He started to get out of his chair.

"Why don't you just stay there and watch TV, and I'll put the potatoes on."

He settled back into his seat. As I walked away, the TV volume went up.

Candy followed me into the kitchen. The potatoes were still soaking in a pot on the stove. I turned on the burner. There was a tin of meat on the counter that was going to go with the potatoes. I'd just open it, cut it into pieces and...

I looked over at the foil package I'd dropped onto the counter. I was really looking forward to having that chicken parm for lunch the next day. It would be a real change from the jam sandwich I always had. But I also knew my father would enjoy it. I picked up the can of meat and put it back on the shelf.

✳

I sat down on the couch, and we watched TV while we ate. I'd studied a bit while the potatoes were boiling. I'd finish my homework before bed or maybe get up early the next day and finish it. Probably both. I couldn't afford to let anybody get ahead of me.

It felt good now to just sit here and to hear my father laugh.

"This is good," he said. "What did you say it's called?"

"Chicken parmesan. Mrs. Priamo made it."

"And why did she give it to you?"

"Oh, she said she accidentally made extra and didn't want it to go to waste, that's all," I said.

"Good, because I don't want you taking things like we're some sort of charity case."

"How was work today?" I asked, changing the subject.

"Not good. Being up half the night is hard."

"Yeah, I know," I mumbled under my breath. I wanted to say, *So I guess you didn't die after all*, but I knew better than that.

"I think they're going to fire me," my father said.

"What? Did your boss say that?"

"He didn't need to say it. I could tell by the way people were looking at me."

"But nobody said anything, right?"

"Weren't you listening?" he snapped. "I can *tell*. I know people."

"But Mr. Campbell is your friend." Mr. Campbell was also his boss.

"Friends come and go. You can't count on them. You can't count on anybody but yourself. Don't ever forget that. Counting on people is counting on being disappointed."

I didn't agree with most things my father said, but this I agreed with. In the end it was up to you.

You couldn't count on anybody to be there. Not friends. Not family. Nobody but yourself.

"If they do fire you, you'll get another job."

"Jobs don't grow on trees, you know."

"Unless you're a lumberjack."

"What did you say?" he asked.

*Uh-oh.* "It was a joke," I said, trying to keep things light. "You know, lumberjacks have jobs because trees grow."

"It's not much of a joke if you have to explain it. Can't you ever take things seriously?"

I was stunned. Everybody who knew me thought I was too serious. Serious was how I took everything. Serious was how I *had* to take everything.

"We're going to have to cut down on things and save some money," he said.

"What are we going to cut down on?" I was worried.

"We'll spend less on groceries, maybe turn the heat down some more, and we won't be buying anything extra."

What extras did he think we were buying now? How much less food could we have? And this place was already freezing.

"We'll be fine," I said. I was talking to myself more than him. "We'll get by."

Candy jumped up onto the couch beside me and put her head in my lap. She was always there to try to make me feel better. But I had a sudden terrible thought. Was her dog food one of those extras we couldn't afford? I'd make sure she ate even if I didn't. I'd take care of her.

I got up and took the empty plate from my father.

"Didn't you mention something about having a test today?"

"Yeah." I was surprised he'd remembered.

"And how did you do?"

"I got the top mark in the class."

"I wouldn't expect any less. Do you have the test with you?"

"It's in my pack."

"Go and get it."

Another surprise. He was interested in something that wasn't about him. Something that was about *me*. Why?

I took our plates into the kitchen and put them in the sink along with the breakfast dishes I hadn't had time to do that morning. I'd do them before I went upstairs.

My pack was on the counter, and I grabbed it and brought it into the living room. I fished out the test and shyly handed it to him.

Slowly he unfolded it and stared at it. "Thirty-three out of thirty-five. You got two answers wrong then. Not perfect."

"Nobody got a perfect score. I told you I got the top mark in the class."

"That just shows that you have a stupid class. Don't go bragging about your marks until they're worth bragging about."

He took the test, crumbled it into a ball and tossed it into the corner.

I felt my knees buckle a little. I should have known better. I always tried to prepare myself, but never knew what was coming. Maybe if I'd gotten perfect…

Next time I'd get perfect.

I turned and walked away. There were dishes to be washed and studying to be done. I'd fallen behind today. Tomorrow I'd have to work harder. Harder than anybody else.

~~1,626~~ 1,625

# SIX

I slept right through the night, only waking up when I heard my father's car door slamming in the morning. He was off to work. I turned off the alarm before it could ring. I'd been worried about him getting enough sleep and worried about him going to work today. His taking an evening nap the night before was usually a bad sign for one or the other or both.

There were lots of times he'd woken me up in the middle of the night, and most of them weren't deliberate. He was often just doing something that had struck him as essential at three in the morning. He could be that way when he was too "up." He might decide to paint a room or rearrange all the furniture or build something in the basement. Usually he only got halfway through the project, leaving me to try to finish it or clean up the mess.

When he did things like that it was disturbing, but at least he was inside the house. Sometimes, though, he'd start up the lawn mower and cut the grass by flashlight, or do a building project in the backyard. That had caused more than one yelling match with neighbors and almost a fist fight once with Mr. Delmonte, who lived behind us. I'd gone out in my pajamas and settled that one down before the two of them came to blows.

My father didn't really talk to any of the neighbors. They exchanged polite nods coming or going, but mostly they didn't bother us and we didn't bother them. I had a pretty good idea that they thought he was nuts, or a jerk. Me, they just felt sorry for. Sometimes I did too.

Living with my father was like being on an elevator—an express elevator. There was the bottom floor and the penthouse, and no stops in between. When he was at the top, everything was perfect and positive and possible. He wouldn't—or I guess couldn't—stop talking and laughing, and he didn't seem to need to even sleep.

He would wake me up to talk or he'd just leave the house and go for a drive. One time he was gone for three days before I heard anything from him. I had no idea where he had gone until I got a telephone call. He was halfway across the country, and it had suddenly dawned on him that he should let me know where he was and that he was on his way home.

It had been another three days before he got back. By then I was almost out of food. There'd been nobody to take care of me and nobody to help. It was just me and Candy. Thank goodness for Candy. I'd been scared. Not just of being alone but also of whether he was ever going to come back. That had happened almost two years ago. Now I was older, we had a bigger supply of food around the house, and I had a job and could buy my own food if I needed to. I knew where he kept extra envelopes of money in the house, and now I even had the password to the bank account. And I had a plan. Actually, I had more than one plan.

He'd lost his job that time. You don't not show up for work for a week and expect you won't get fired. He'd lost lots of jobs. Sometimes it was for swearing at the boss or taking a swing at somebody or telling everybody that they were stupid. Sometimes it was for being so "off" he couldn't do the job. It was strange, but I didn't worry as much about his losing so many jobs as I did about the other stuff. He always seemed to be able to get another job. He was just as good at getting hired as he was at getting fired. First impressions he was usually good at.

When he came down in that elevator from the penthouse, he would plummet to the bottom floor. Not the main lobby. More like the parking garage, five floors below the surface. That's where the elevator door opened. Not at middle floors. Either way too high or way too low.

In the parking garage, suddenly the world was dark and silent. All the positivity was gone, and days might go by where he hardly said a word. He'd barely move except to go to work. Sometimes he didn't go to work at all. He'd only eat when I brought him food and he'd rarely get out of bed. And he'd cry. I hated it when he cried, more than almost anything in the world. I hated his tears even more than I hated jam sandwiches.

Whether he was up or down, I had no choice but to wait for the elevator to move again. I lived waiting, watching, as his finger hovered over the button. When he was up, I wanted him down, and when he was down, I wanted him up.

When I was younger, I thought he was like that because of me. I finally realized he wasn't.

I also used to think that I could control his behavior by doing the right things. But I was even more wrong about that. It was *his* finger, his button, his elevator and his building. I was only along for the ride. Sometimes I wondered if my mother just got so tired of it all that she wanted to get off the elevator. Could somebody will themselves to die? Was that possible?

In the brief time when the elevator was racing between the top and the bottom, we passed the middle floors. Those were the places where normal people lived. That was where I wanted to live.

The night before had been normal. I'd slept all the way through. It would have been wonderful if my father had done the laundry. I should have done it before I went to bed instead of having to do it now. As always, I made my lunch. As always it was the same lunch, but today I made two jam sandwiches and grabbed two apples. We didn't have any more bananas. I was going to take twice as much in case Harmony had decided to continue her hunger strike at home and needed a lunch.

That was assuming she was even at school today. Maybe she'd decided to run away last night. That was possible—and, if she had, probably better for me. Still, I wanted to be ready for whatever. I couldn't help but think how much nicer it would have been to share the chicken parmesan with Harmony than giving it to my father. Was it mean of me to think that way? He had really enjoyed it.

I grabbed some clothes out of the dryer. The T-shirt I chose was still a little damp in the collar, but it was longer than the others. That meant I could wear my pants lower on my hips, which meant the bottoms would be a bit closer to the ground.

My pants were clean, but they hadn't gotten any longer in the wash.

Before leaving the house I went through the checklist in my head—eat breakfast, make my lunch, cleanup, dress, walk Candy. All done, and the laundry too, and I'd read four chapters of the book for my report. I'd already read the whole novel once, but I always liked to go through a book twice. It wasn't like it was a bad thing—I really did like reading. Sometimes if the book was good it was more real than real life. It was also an escape from real life. Funny how nobody I read about was ever going through what I was going through. In some ways that was reassuring.

I realized there was one thing I hadn't put in my bag. I grabbed the pack and went into the living room. There it was in the corner, all balled up. The crumpled test. I put the pack down and tried to flatten out the paper. I needed a signature from a parent. That was Mr. Yeoman's standard. He said if you weren't doing well, he wanted your parents to know, and if you were doing well, he wanted them to know even more.

I pulled a pen out of my bag and tried again to flatten out the crinkles in the paper. I held the pen in my left hand—the hand my father used—and very carefully added his signature. I'd signed his signature on so many things already that the only way anybody at school would be suspicious was if my father actually did sign something.

Then I decided to add something besides the signature—a comment.

*I'm very proud of Robbie. Keep up the good work!*

I felt a shudder go through my entire body. That's what he should have said. That's what parents wrote when they weren't too busy taking elevator rides and were actually acting like parents and caring for their kids the way parents were supposed to.

I folded up the test and tucked it in my pack. I gave Candy another pat on the head and slammed the door shut, making sure it was locked. I bounced across the porch, down the stairs, along the walk and—

"Good morning!"

I spun around, practically jumping in the air. Harmony was sitting on my porch.

"What are you doing here?" I sputtered.

"It's called sitting, and I think the correct response to me saying good morning is that you say good morning back."

"Okay, good morning."

"You look surprised to see me."

"I'd be pretty surprised to see anybody sitting on my porch."

"I thought this would be the best place to wait." She looked at her watch. "If you hadn't come out in a few minutes, I was going to knock."

"I think that's the normal procedure."

"There's not much normal about me, Robert. I thought a smart guy like you would have figured that out fairly quickly. We better get going or we might be late."

"We have plenty of time."

"But don't you like to be early?" she asked.

"Um…yeah…did I mention that to you?"

"No, but do you think you're the only smart person around here?" She bounced down the stairs and past me. "Try to keep up."

I fell in beside her.

"So you decided not to run away," I said.

"Or I decided I wanted you to come along with me, and we could run off together."

I startled slightly.

"Just joking. Don't take everything so seriously. Yes, I decided to stick around...at least for today."

We started walking, but then I began to feel anxious. Harmony had startled me so much that I couldn't remember whether I'd made sure the door was locked. It had to be. It always was the times I'd gone back to check. But the thought kept rattling around in my head. Had I *really* locked the door? Probably. Probably wasn't good enough. If I didn't check, it would be in my head all day.

"Hang on," I said. I ran back, jumped up the stairs and tried the door. It was locked. Of course it was locked. I jogged back to her.

"I wasn't sure I'd locked the door," I explained.

"And had you?"

I nodded. "I just like to be careful."

"Interesting," she said. "So now that you've checked, you're sure it's locked, right?"

"I just checked it!"

"And you're completely certain, 100 percent positive, that it's locked?"

If the door weren't locked and someone went inside, Candy would rip them to shreds. She didn't like strangers.

"Yes, it's locked."

"That yes didn't sound so certain. Don't you think you should go back and check it again?"

I slowed down slightly, looked back over my shoulder at the house and—

"It's locked!" Harmony yelled.

I nodded.

"There's a fine line between being careful and being paranoid. If you go back again, you've crossed that line."

"I'm not going back." Even if I wanted to, I couldn't now. "How did you know where I live?"

"I followed you home and slept on your porch last night."

"You followed me?…Oh, you're joking."

"Of course I'm joking. You told me your address when we walked home."

"Oh yeah, that's right."

"I remember things. I watch and I listen." She turned slightly so that she was looking at me as we walked. "But so do you."

"What do you mean?"

"You spend your life watching and listening. You probably can't help yourself." She laughed.

"Maybe I'm just naturally observant," I replied. I felt uncomfortable, like I was under a microscope. "Did you eat breakfast today?" I asked, eager to change the subject.

"Blueberry pancakes. I couldn't resist."

"And should I assume you also brought lunch?"

"Packed and in my bag."

I was relieved but also a little sad. I realized I'd been looking forward to sharing with her.

"Was your mother able to get the blood out of your T-shirt?" Harmony asked.

I gave her an answer without talking about what I didn't want to talk about. "It came out."

"Good. I would have felt bad if I had ruined it. You don't have a lot of clothing, do you?"

"What?"

"You don't have a lot of clothing. Am I wrong?"

I didn't answer. I didn't know how to answer.

"Look, nothing to be ashamed of. It's just that these pants you're wearing today are better than the ones you were wearing yesterday, but they're too short as well. I figure if you had a lot of clothes, you'd have picked a pair that was longer, because I really did give you a hard time about it yesterday."

I didn't want her to know how much that had bothered me or that I'd deliberately tried to pick a longer pair.

"Did you just go through a growth spurt?" Harmony asked.

"Yeah, I'm growing fast."

"Outgrowing your clothes and they haven't been replaced. Are you poor?"

"What sort of a question is that?"

"Seems pretty straightforward. I'm poor. Are you?"

"My father has a job."

"Most poor people have jobs. You never heard the term *working poor*?" she asked.

"I've heard it."

"It's just that if you're poor, that would explain why nobody's spending money on clothes for you. Do your mother and father dress better than you do?"

I was stunned. I didn't know what to say. And once again she'd mentioned my mother. Did she know about my mom being dead and was just being mean, or was she testing me, or did it mean nothing?

"Don't take this so personal. It's not like I have great clothes. My mother doesn't even have a job. I'm living in a foster home because she couldn't care for me. I'm just wondering, that's all."

"Maybe you should wonder less."

"Are you telling me to shut up?"

"Would it work?" I asked.

"Probably not…but I'll stop if I can ask you one more question."

She stepped in front of me and put her hands on my shoulders. For a split second I thought she was going to punch me again. She looked me right in the eyes and asked, "Before I waste any more of my time on you, are we going to be friends?"

That was *not* what I had expected. Neither was my answer. "I thought we already were friends."

"Friends don't lie," she said.

"But lying to the principal about what happened proved that I'm your friend, didn't it?"

"I'm not talking about lying to him. I'm talking about lying to me."

"What are you talking about? I haven't lied to you about anything."

"Yes, you have. You did it yesterday and you did it just now."

"And what exactly did I say that was a lie?"

"You can tell lies by what people say, but you can also tell lies by what they *don't* say."

I shook my head and let out a deep sigh. This girl was nothing but confusion. "Are you going to explain this to me?"

"I made comments about your mother…a few times."

"Yeah, so what?"

"She doesn't live with you, does she?"

"What makes you think that?" So she didn't know the truth.

"Look, my mother is a drunk and a druggie and even she wouldn't send me out in those clothes and that lunch you had yesterday."

I felt like I'd been punched in the stomach. It felt worse than actually getting hit in the nose.

"Look, there's no shame in only having one parent around."

That wasn't what I felt. Lots of people didn't live with both of their parents. For some reason I felt ashamed that I was the only one who didn't *have* a mother because she had died.

"Have they been divorced for a long time?" she asked.

"They aren't divorced," I said.

"Separated or not married to begin with?"

"They were married."

"So she just took off? My mother ran away a couple of times too."

"My mother didn't run away." *I guess in one way she did.*

She looked puzzled. "So…your parents were married. But they didn't get divorced, and she didn't run away. But she isn't there anymore."

She leaned closer and stared harder into my eyes. I wanted to look away, I wanted to break away, but I was powerless to do either.

"So that must mean...oh, she's *dead*."

I nodded ever so slightly.

"Look...I'm sorry...I didn't know." Harmony almost seemed upset. "It's just that sometimes I'm a big mouthy idiot who thinks she's smarter than she is and who should just keep her mouth closed and stop being such a jerk who—"

"You're not a jerk!" I snapped, cutting her off. "It's just that I don't like talking about it. That's all."

"How long ago did it happen? When did she die?"

"I told you I don't want to talk about it! What part of that didn't you get?"

Tears started to form in the corners of her eyes. I felt bad. But I just wanted to be left alone.

"Look, I'm sorry about your mother," she said.

"Me too. It's just...just...it's hard."

"And I shouldn't have made you talk about it. I'm sorry."

I had the strangest urge to tell her that my grandparents had died too, but I decided not to. I never talked to people about that.

"Do you still want to be friends?" she asked.

"Do I have a choice?" I hoped she could tell by my voice that I wasn't really mad.

She smiled. "Not really."

"Then I guess we're friends."

# SEVEN

At lunchtime we sat with my friends. Harmony had asked if she could, and I'd checked with the guys to make sure it was okay. I didn't expect anybody to object, and I told them it would probably only be for that day or a couple of days at most, until she found some other friends. She'd gotten to know a couple of the girls in our class, but she said she'd rather sit with us because girls were "too much work and too much drama." I almost laughed out loud when she said that because to me she seemed to be the queen of drama.

I could tell that both Jay and Raj were a little uncomfortable. Girls made them nervous. Not that Taylor or Sal or I was in any way smooth or cool, but at least we could make words come out of our mouths when we were around girls.

"Okay, do you guys want me to sit here or not?" Harmony asked.

We all exchanged looks. "Sure," Taylor said.

"Of course," Jay added, and the others nodded or mumbled agreement.

"Then all of you have to stop fiddling with your phones," she said.

Raj and Sal had been playing games on their phones, and Taylor had his in his hand. He always had his phone in his hand when he wasn't in class. I didn't blame him. He had a new model with a big screen. In a neighborhood without much money, his family had more than most.

"I'm not going to sit here and be ignored," Harmony said. "I don't do well being ignored."

Nothing dramatic about that.

"Put your phones right there, right in the middle of the table," she ordered.

Before Taylor could react, she reached out and took his phone away from him. He looked shocked. She placed it right in the center of the table.

"Now the rest of you," she directed.

Raj put his phone right beside Taylor's. Sal did too, followed by Jay. None of their phones were as big or nice as Taylor's.

"How about you?" she asked me.

"I don't have a phone."

"Really?"

"Nope," Taylor said. "You call him at home or you don't call him at all."

"I don't know how he does it," Raj added.

"My father doesn't have a cell phone either. He doesn't really believe in them," I said.

"That's a new trend some people are following," Harmony said. "I think they call it *unplugging*."

I didn't know about trends. What I did know was that two years back—when he was on one of his highs—my father had run up a phone bill of thousands of dollars. He'd refused to pay it off, and nobody was going to give him—or me—a cell phone until he did.

"I've heard of people unplugging," Taylor said. "I just don't think I could do it."

"*You* probably couldn't," Harmony said. "Some people need a fancy phone to make themselves feel important."

Taylor looked hurt. This was uncomfortable. I wanted to fix that. "Just so you know, Taylor, if you ever want to unplug, I would love to have your phone. It's the best."

He looked relieved.

"At least Robbie has a computer," Sal said.

"Everybody has a computer," I said.

"I don't," Harmony said. "And I don't have a phone either. I like to be in the here and now. So do you want to trade some lunch?" she asked me, opening her pack and pulling out a lunch bag.

"Depends what you have," I replied. But I knew I would take pretty much anything.

"It's going to be good," she promised. "What do you have?"

"He always has jam sandwiches!" Taylor exclaimed.

"He's the king of jam sandwiches!" Sal added, and everybody laughed.

"Every day, five days a week!" Taylor added.

I'd never talked about it, and neither had anybody else before this. Obviously it was a running joke. Was I a running joke as well?

"I happen to like jam sandwiches," Harmony said. "Especially Robert's sandwiches."

They all looked at each other. I knew what was coming.

"*Robert*?" Taylor said.

"Aren't we getting a bit formal?" Jay added.

"I told her to call me Robbie."

"But I'm going to call him Robert because that's what I want to call him. Anybody have anything else they want to say about that?" Harmony asked.

She looked at each of us in turn. Jay and Raj looked down at the table. This girl had a serious glare. They didn't even know about her capacity for inflicting physical damage, and they were still afraid of her.

Taylor held up his hands in surrender. "You can call him whatever you want, but how do you know that *Robert* has good sandwiches?"

"Because I forgot my lunch yesterday and he was nice enough to share his with me."

There was a collective *ooooooh* and lots of waggling eyebrows from the guys.

"What is this, the second grade or the eighth?" Harmony asked.

They shut up. It had taken all of two minutes for them to figure out she wasn't to be messed with. I liked that. And didn't like it. All at once.

"Mr. Yeoman told him to watch out for me," Harmony said. "Robert really didn't have a choice. Giving me part of his lunch was almost an order, if you think about it."

They nodded in agreement. I knew she was just trying to get me off the hook.

"And we all know that Robbie always does what teachers tell him," Raj said.

"And you don't?" Harmony asked.

"Well...mostly," he admitted.

"Then maybe you should just button it."

Harmony pulled out a sandwich, two bananas and a couple of pears.

"Roast beef on whole wheat," she said to me. "Do you want to trade half of this for half of yours?"

"I don't know."

"You don't like roast beef?" she asked.

"Of course I do."

"Then you should take it. It's rude to turn some-body down. Besides, I want a jam sandwich." She unwrapped her sandwich and put half of it down in front of me.

"Thank you," I said. "You can have a whole one if you want. I packed two…you know…in case."

"In case I didn't bring my lunch?" she asked.

I nodded.

"That's so, so…thoughtful," Harmony said.

"And *sweet*," Taylor said. "Don't you think it's sweet, guys?"

"Are we back in second grade again?" Harmony asked. She looked from one to the other, glaring. "Anybody have anything they want to say?"

They remained silent, and even the smirk on Raj's face vanished.

I pulled out my two sandwiches and the two apples and handed her one of each. She gave me a banana and a pear. I almost said no but stopped myself. There was no point in arguing with her. That much I already knew. Besides, why would I?

"This guy makes the best jam sandwiches in the entire world!" Harmony exclaimed as she unwrapped it and took a big bite. "Maybe he *is* the king of jam sandwiches."

When she said it, it didn't sound like an accusation. I picked up her sandwich. It was made of that fancy kind of bread with seeds. There were lettuce, tomatoes and some sort of mayo on it. And roast beef. We *never* had roast beef. My father used to buy bologna sometimes, but that had stopped a long time ago.

"Good afternoon."

I turned around. It was Mr. Snow. He taught science and was also the coach of the basketball team. I'd sort of been avoiding him.

"Robbie, what are these rumors I'm hearing that you're not going to be trying out for my team?"

"I guess they're more than rumors, sir. I'm not going to try out."

"Is it because you don't like the coach?" he asked.

I almost answered before I realized he was joking. "No, sir, of course not. It's just that I can't.

I have a job after school. I work at the Priamo butcher shop."

"Every day?" he asked.

"Monday, Thursday, every Saturday and some Fridays as well."

"And he won't let you take some time off during the basketball season?"

"I really don't want to ask him."

"I could talk to your father or even Mr. Priamo himself. Did you know that his youngest son, the one who just got married, used to be on my team?"

"I didn't know that. But I don't think I want you to talk to anybody."

He gave me an intense look. "Are you sure?"

I nodded.

"It's just that since your growth spurt, I pretty well had you penciled in at center."

Wow. He wanted me to play center? "Sorry," I said. I just didn't think I could swing it.

"What if he came out for as many of the practices and games as he could?" Harmony asked.

"And you are…?" Mr. Snow asked.

"Harmony. I'm new here."

"Hello, Harmony. I'm afraid that's not how a team works. It wouldn't be fair to his teammates who are always there," he replied.

"Don't you think the team could decide that? Anybody here at this table trying out for the team?" Harmony asked.

Raj and Taylor raised their hands.

"Would either of you be upset about Robert only being there when he could, because of work?"

"I'd like him there all the time," Taylor said, "but I'd rather have him with us when he could than not at all."

Sal and Jay—who were not basketball players— nodded in agreement, as did Raj.

"Well, Coach?"

"Hmm. Perhaps you're onto something, Harmony. Robbie, do you think you could try to get a day off or shift to another day if there was a game? Or even go in a little later that day?" he asked.

"I guess I could try." I would talk to Mrs. Priamo. She might let me.

"Then we have a deal?" Harmony asked Mr. Snow.

"I'll have to check with the other players, but this could work. We might have to make this a two-parter though. We need a student manager. Harmony, would you be willing to take on that role?"

"Sounds like blackmail," she replied.

"Sounds more to me like a negotiation. So? What do you say?"

She looked at me.

"Go for it," I said.

"I guess we have a deal."

The bell rang, and Mr. Snow hurried off. He had class. As did we. The rest of the guys jumped up, but I hesitated, trying to finish my pear. Harmony stayed behind too.

"You did want to play basketball, right?" she asked.

"Yeah, definitely," I replied. "I just didn't think I could swing it. I guess I should thank you."

"No guessing involved. You *should* thank me, but I should also thank you for the lunch."

"I got the better end of that trade," I said.

"You did, but you didn't know that when you packed your lunch. You were thinking of me and went and made extra in case I needed it."

"It was just an apple and a jam sandwich."

"It doesn't matter what it was. You were thinking of me. That doesn't happen to me very often." She paused and looked directly at me. "But then again, it doesn't happen to you much either, does it?"

I nodded ever so slightly. I wanted to say *never*.

The guys were standing at the door and waved for us to join them.

"We have to get to class," I said instead.

# EIGHT

There was a loud knock on the door. Candy went crazy. Her nails scratched and skidded on the floor as she tried to gain traction while racing for the door, howling and growling and barking as she ran. I put down my pen, pushed aside my math homework and ran to see who was there. When I got to the door, Candy was jumping up and against it. I never had to worry about somebody sneaking into the house. She made me feel safe. Well, safer.

I grabbed her by the collar, pulled her down and peered through the window in the door to see who was outside. It was Harmony. What was she doing here?

I opened the door slightly, still holding Candy by the collar, and pushed the dog back as I squeezed through the opening and then closed the door shut behind me.

"She doesn't like people," I explained.

"Dogs like me."

"She doesn't like anybody."

"She'd like me. I'm special," Harmony said.

"No question you're special, but she'd still take a special chunk out of you. What are you doing here?" I asked.

"You could try to be more welcoming than your dog. How about starting with something like 'Hello. How are you doing? So nice to see you!'"

"Um, sure. Hello, nice to see you, and how are you doing?"

"Better, but not convincing. You work, so I assume you must have some money."

Was she running away and needed some bucks to help her get wherever she was going?

"I have some money," I said carefully. "How much do you need?"

She looked insulted. "Do you think I came over here to borrow money from you?"

I was thrown—but not completely. My father had given me plenty of practice in recovering from the unexpected.

"I didn't think you wanted money," I said quickly. "I wanted you to know that I'm here if you did, you know, need some money for something important."

"It is important. We need to go shopping," she said.

"You want me to go shopping with you?"

"You have it backward. *I'm* going to go shopping with *you* for a pair of pants that don't show your ankles. Do you have enough money for that?"

"Yeah, probably."

"Good, and if you didn't, I was going to loan *you* a few bucks," she said.

"I'm okay."

"So. Can we go shopping?"

I went through the checklist in my head. I'd peeled the potatoes and put them on the stove, ready to boil. I'd walked Candy. I'd straightened up the place. I'd even done most of my math homework.

"We can do that."

"Then why don't you lock the door, check three or four times that it's really locked, and we'll go."

* ★

"Try these on!" Mrs. Levy said from outside the cubicle as she passed another pair of pants over the top of the changeroom door.

Levy's Discount Department Store was a little place on Rogers Road, just up the street from my house. Mrs. Levy and her husband ran the place. One of their kids, Augie, was a couple of years older than me. They were nice people.

I looked at the pants. They were sort of casual and sort of formal. They were fancier than what I usually wore, which probably meant more expensive.

"Are you decent in there?" Harmony called out.

"Not yet."

"Then hurry up. I want to see."

I pulled them on and did up the zipper and the top button. They fit pretty well in the waist. Not too tight.

I walked out and Harmony was standing right there. "What do you think of them?" she asked. "And before you answer, I want you to know that I personally and specifically selected them."

"They are, without a doubt, the most perfect, beautiful pair of pants in the whole store. Maybe in the whole world."

"Robert, sarcasm does not suit you. Now come and let's have a better look."

I stepped up onto a little wooden bench and did a slight turn as Harmony and Mrs. Levy looked and made comments. Mrs. Levy tugged down on the legs slightly. My big toes were sticking out of little holes in my socks. I wished I'd worn another pair.

"Not a bad length," she said.

"His ankles are completely covered," Harmony agreed.

Mrs. Levy grabbed them—grabbed me—by the waistband. "They are a good fit, although you really need to gain a little weight."

"That seems to be the common opinion," Harmony said.

This was the seventh pair of pants I'd tried on, so I was starting to feel less uncomfortable being stared at and prodded like a prize pig.

"How much hem do they have?" Harmony asked.

Before Mrs. Levy could answer, Harmony grabbed me, almost knocking me off balance, and rolled up the bottom of one pant leg.

"That's good," Mrs. Levy said. "There's enough to let down maybe an inch and a half if he gets taller before the pants wear out."

"And if he bought them, would you be able to do that?" Harmony asked.

"His mother could easily do it."

"No, she couldn't," Harmony said. "His mother died."

I felt my whole body stiffen. The air was still and silent, Harmony's words just hanging there. I didn't often tell people about my mother, and when I did this was always the response. It made both me and the person who'd just found out uncomfortable.

"I'm so sorry. Did it happen recently?"

I shook my head. "A long time ago. I was four."

"Too young. Far too young." Mrs. Levy shook her head.

I felt even worse now. And a bit mad. Harmony had no right to make either of us feel this way.

"You come back when they need to be let down, and I'll do it for you. All part of the deal."

"I don't know if we have a deal yet," Harmony said. "What sort of discount are you offering?"

"Discount?"

"You know, some sort of friends-and-family discount."

"Well, I know you're not family, because I've never seen you around my kitchen table for dinner or at the holidays, and although you've been friendly, I don't think you quite qualify as my friends yet."

"We'll be good friends if you give us a good discount."

I couldn't believe how bold Harmony was being. Was Mrs. Levy going to be offended or—

Mrs. Levy laughed. "Okay, how about 10 percent?"

"I was hoping we'd be better friends. How about 20 percent?"

"I don't give my real family 20 percent. Let's split the difference and go with 15," said Mrs. Levy. "I'll throw in a pair of socks that don't have holes."

The holes were impossible to miss as I stood there without shoes.

Harmony looked up at me. "Well?"

I nodded.

"Deal."

I was wearing my new pants and socks. They felt good. I felt good. Mrs. Levy put my old clothes in a bag. I had the feeling she wanted to put them in the garbage, but I'd still need them. The old pants would be good for times I didn't want to risk damaging the new ones, and those socks, even with the holes, weren't the worst ones I owned.

"Here you go, dear," she said as she handed me the bag.

"Thank you."

The look in her eyes, the tone in her voice, had changed when she found out about my mother.

I'd seen and heard it before. It most often came from women, especially those who were mothers. It was probably part of what got me the discount and the free socks. I wanted those, but I didn't want what went with them. I didn't feel comfortable. I didn't want a hand on my shoulder or their pity. Or the shame I felt. I had to talk to Harmony later and tell her not to do that again.

"You must be so pleased with how handsome your boyfriend looks in his new pants," Mrs. Levy said to Harmony.

Harmony and I exchanged a quick look.

"You two are so sweet to each other. You fit together. It's so lovely," Mrs. Levy added.

"Thank you," Harmony said.

She looked at me and gave a slight shake of the head. I got the message to stay quiet.

We said our goodbyes and left. Harmony was unusually silent. I wasn't saying anything either. I wasn't really sure what to say or where to start—at Mrs. Levy thinking we were boyfriend and girlfriend, or Harmony mentioning my mother. So I went with something simple to break the silence.

"Let me guess. Your favorite TV show is *Let's Make A Deal*?"

"I know about having to make deals to survive."

I nodded in agreement. I'd made my share of deals.

"Have you ever made a deal with God?" Harmony asked.

"What?"

"You know, like, a 'Hey, God, if you make my mother stop drinking, I'll try to do better in school' sort of deal."

Once again this girl had just punched me in the face without raising a fist.

"Well, have you?" she asked.

"Why would you think that?"

"I just figured because your mother died…"

Apparently this wasn't going to be simple in any way. "I was only four when she died."

"Yeah, you mentioned that to Mrs. Levy. I'm sorry. I didn't know you were that young. It must have been really hard, losing her when you were so little."

"Maybe it was easier, but I know what you mean."

"So what sort of deals do you make with God?" she asked.

I hadn't told her I made *any*, but she was right. "About being patient and not complaining if my father doesn't come home at night."

She looked shocked. I was even more shocked that I'd said it. I'd never told anybody about him leaving me alone all night sometimes. I shouldn't have started this, but the words had just popped out. What did I say now?

"That sounds like my mother. Sometimes she wouldn't roll in until midnight or later."

Her understanding of what I meant wasn't as bad as the truth. I nodded again.

"A couple of times, when she was on a real bender, it was so late that I thought she wasn't coming home at all."

"That would be awful." It *was* awful.

"Being left alone is spooky," she said.

"I have Candy."

"Does that make it better?"

"Much better. At least nobody is ever going to sneak in while she's around."

THE KING OF JAM SANDWICHES · ✳ 111

"How often does he do that, go out and leave you?"

"Not that often," I lied. Even once was too much.

"My mother and your father," she said, shaking her head. "What sort of person would do that to their kid?"

I'd asked myself that question more than once. And Harmony didn't know the whole truth.

"You are one strong guy, Robert."

"No stronger than you. You do what you have to do, right?"

"Yes, you do. You've got to. You understand it. Do you still make deals with God?"

"No. Not anymore."

"Because you don't believe there is a God?" she asked.

I shook my head. "I believe. I just don't ask for things." Asking for something just means getting turned down and disappointed. Better not to even bother asking for better.

She grabbed my arm and spun me around with such suddenness and force that I was shocked.

"If there is a God, I don't think he cares," she said, her voice low and quiet like she didn't want to be overheard, though there was nobody around us.

"Why are you whispering?"

"If God does exist, I don't want him to hear me. There's no point in getting him any madder at us than he already is."

"Okay." That actually made sense.

We started walking again. More silence. The silence made me uncomfortable. I decided I'd break it in a big way.

"That was pretty strange about Mrs. Levy thinking we were a couple," I said.

"It *was* strange. But I don't want you to get the wrong idea just because I went with you to get clothes. I'm not looking for a boyfriend."

"And I'm not looking for a girlfriend!" I exclaimed.

She looked at me for a moment. "Are you, you know, gay?"

"Not that it's any of your business, but no, I'm not."

"I just wondered," she said.

We walked for a while without saying a word.

"Is it because of your mother dying?" she finally asked. "Is that why you don't want a girlfriend?"

I didn't know what to say to that.

"When a parent dies or leaves, there are often unresolved feelings that get directed toward others. You lost your mother, so maybe you have a distrust of women."

"Are you insane?"

"You'd be surprised."

"Where do you even get ideas like that?" I asked.

"My social worker says that because my father was never there, I likely have issues with men."

"You have a social worker?"

"I've had lots of social workers. I'm in foster care. Do you think they'd give me an electrician? If I have issues with men, then you might have issues with women. Doesn't that make sense?"

"I don't have issues with anybody," I said.

"Are you sure? Because I have issues with almost *everybody*."

"Yeah, big secret."

"So why don't you want a girlfriend?"

"I don't want a girlfriend because I just don't have time for one."

"They don't take up much time."

"More time than I have. You don't understand," I said. This was getting really irritating.

"Then explain it."

"If I did tell you, you'd think I was strange."

"Oh, Robert. Your being strange is one of the things I like best about you. It's why we're friends. Just tell me."

I stopped walking. I took a seat on the steps of a walk leading up to a house. Harmony stood right in front of me. I had to decide exactly what I was going to tell her or if I *should* tell her anything. She had blurted about me and my mother to Mrs. Levy. Would she tell people about this too?

"If I tell you, you can't tell anybody," I finally said.

"I won't."

"Okay, like I said, this is going to sound strange." I took a deep breath. "I get up every morning knowing that I have to work hard."

"That's no surprise."

"Not just hard. *Harder*. I get up thinking that I need to work harder and longer than everybody in the entire world, and if I do that, I can gain just a little. And if I do that every day, day after day after day, eventually I might, well, become somebody." There. I'd said it. She stood there looking down at me.

"I know it sounds stupid but—"

"It doesn't sound stupid at all. It makes complete sense," she said, nodding. "Except you're wrong about one thing."

"What?" I asked.

"Robert, you already *are* somebody."

"What?"

"You already are somebody."

And that's when I burst into tears.

# NINE

We sat at my kitchen table and sipped cups of tea. I would have offered her something else, but tea and water were all we had in the house. I'd locked Candy in the bathroom, and she'd finally settled down. She only yipped once in a while. It had taken her much longer to settle down and stop barking and growling than it had for me to stop crying. But I hadn't stopped feeling bad and *very* embarrassed. I'd known this girl for only two days, and I'd started crying in front of her. The only thing that made it better—or worse—in any way was that Harmony had started crying too. That had shocked me.

I glanced at my watch. Five thirty. Still safe. My father wouldn't be home for at least another half hour. Depending on traffic, maybe even an hour. Of course, sometimes it wasn't the traffic and he didn't get home until nine or ten at night. Those were the times I wondered if he was going to come home at all. None of that mattered now. I just needed to get Harmony out of here before he arrived. But I needed to say something first.

"I want to apologize to you."

"For what?" she asked.

"For getting so upset earlier."

"I cried too," she said. "How about if we just pretend it never happened?"

"Sounds good. Thanks."

"That's what friends do." She paused. "You might not know this, but I don't have many friends."

I almost said, *Big surprise*, but I stopped myself. "It's probably hard to make friends when you keep moving around."

"It's not that. It's just that, well, I don't have that much in common with kids my age."

"I get it. When I'm talking to you, it's like talking to somebody older," I said.

"I feel the same way. But usually when people say things like that, it feels almost like an accusation. *Why don't you act your age? Who are you trying to fool?*"

I laughed. Again I knew exactly what she meant.

"Sometimes I don't just feel old, but old and tired," she said.

"I get tired."

"Do you ever get so tired that you just want to go to sleep?"

"Sometimes I get so tired that I can't sleep," I answered.

"I understand that. Too many thoughts and too much to be worried about. Do you ever want to just go away, never come back, disappear?"

"Disappear. Do you mean, like, *die*?"

"It would be easier." She paused, and I held my breath. "Not that I'd ever hurt myself or anything."

I exhaled. *Thank goodness.*

"Maybe we feel tired because we have to think about things other kids don't have to think about," I said.

"That's probably it. Some people have to be older because of what life gives them. You have to be older just like I do. And so you know, like I said before, I won't tell anybody that you're poor," she said.

"What?"

"I won't tell anybody that you're poor."

"I'm not poor."

Harmony gestured around the room.

"My father just doesn't like to spend money on things."

He didn't like to spend money on *anything*. The last new thing to come into the house had been a dishcloth—two months ago. The old one had been in ribbons.

"I guess that explains why you don't have a cell phone."

"You don't have one either," I said.

"I *had* a phone. My mom hocked it."

"Really?"

"She sold her phone too. That's why I can't get a hold of her now."

"She just took your phone and sold it? That's awful."

"That's not the worst. Sometimes I'd come home from school and find the kettle was gone, or the toaster, or living room furniture, or even some of my toys."

"She'd sell your *toys*?"

"All the time. When I was little I didn't even notice. I just thought I'd lost them. The first time I really noticed was when she sold my favorite toy—a stuffed polar bear."

"That's terrible," I said.

"I always snuggled with it when I went to bed, and one night I couldn't find it. I looked under the bed and under the covers and said I wouldn't go to sleep until we found it. My mother made lots of excuses and then finally admitted what she'd done."

I couldn't imagine how Harmony must have felt—no, wait. I *could* imagine it.

"She told me she'd go and buy it back the next day. That's the only reason I was finally able to get to sleep that night," she said.

"And did she get it back?'

She shook her head. "Of course not, but even that wasn't the worst."

I waited. Wondering, wanting to hear, but also not wanting to hear.

"One Christmas morning I woke up and there were, like, a dozen wrapped presents under the tree."

"How is that bad?"

"I got to open the presents. There was great stuff, and I got to play with it all day."

"Still wondering how that was bad," I said.

"I got to play with it *that* day. The next day she returned it all to the stores. They weren't really my presents."

Harmony laughed, but it wasn't a real laugh. It was sort of a laugh-so-you-don't-cry laugh.

"She'd sell whatever she could to get money for alcohol or drugs. Is that your father's problem too?"

"No. He doesn't drink except for when he goes out on a Saturday night. I don't think I've ever seen him drunk."

"That makes it even more confusing."

"What's so confusing?"

"He has a job, and he doesn't do drugs or drink, and you say he has money, but there's no food in the house."

"We have food."

"I'm not talking about just potatoes and bread and jam for your sandwiches."

"We have different food, and we have *lots* of food."

"Look, I know I shouldn't have, but when you were checking on the dog, I looked in the fridge. It's almost empty, and I bet there's not much in the cupboards either."

She was right. There wasn't much in the cupboards or fridge. But we had food. "We have lots and lots of food."

"You don't have to lie to me."

"I'm not lying." I got to my feet. "Come with me." I went to the basement door, opened it and clicked on the light. "Be careful. The stairs are steep."

I started down, and Harmony followed. As we went, I realized I was not just telling her things I didn't tell people but was now going to show her something I didn't show to anybody.

"Is this the scene where the beautiful, innocent young girl goes into the dark basement and then gets murdered?" she asked.

I looked back at her. "First off, I think you've already proven that you can take me, and second... innocent?"

"I notice you didn't argue the beautiful part."

I didn't know how to answer that. I hit a second light switch, and the far side of the basement became visible.

Harmony gasped. "Wow."

There against the back wall were the shelves. They were almost floor to ceiling, and they were filled with cans and packages of food.

"I told you we had lots of food."

"You didn't tell me you had a grocery store in your basement."

"We just like to be prepared," I said.

"Prepared for what, the zombie apocalypse?"

The shelves were full of tinned meat and cans of peas, corn, carrots, mixed vegetables, peaches and pears. There were glass jars of spaghetti sauce and lots of packages of pasta to go with them. There were dozens of boxes of cereal, packages of crackers and jars of jam and peanut butter. And just to the side of the shelves sat a gigantic bag of potatoes.

"There's enough food down here to feed an army."

"Or two people for six months," I said. *Or one person for a year*.

"But why?"

"It's good to be prepared in case we can't shop."

"You could miss shopping for a few months and be okay. So is this what you do with the money you earn at your job?"

"Nope. My father just stocks up whenever there's a sale."

"Well, I guess there were lots of sales," said Harmony. She grabbed a mega-giant jar of jam. "Enough jam to make sandwiches for the rest of the year! Long live the king!"

I picked up a clipboard. "This is where my father keeps track of all the food we have. It has to be rotated out regularly so it doesn't go bad."

"Canned stuff goes bad?"

"Everything spoils eventually."

She looked at me. "Are you getting philosophical on me?"

"No, I really mean food. Canned stuff can last for years. Packaged spaghetti and noodles too, if they're kept dry. Bread and cereal get stale even if they're sealed. Potatoes start to root or rot. If it goes bad, then we wasted money."

"And your father doesn't like to waste money," she said.

"Only people with lots of money can waste it."

Harmony's gaze went back and forth along the shelves. "What I now don't understand is, if you have this much food, how come you're so skinny?"

"It's here for a reason," I explained.

"And eating it isn't the reason?"

"Eating it takes away the reason."

"I'm thinking the reason is that you and your father are paranoid."

I was going to argue, but she was right. My father and I *were* paranoid, but in different ways. His paranoia had allowed me to convince him we needed this food supply. And we did. At least, I did. I had almost run out of food the time he took off for a week. Now he could be gone for six months and I'd be okay. He could *die* and I'd be okay for six months. Now that I had the banking password,

I could always buy more food. The money I got from my job would help too.

"Do you ever just take a can of something and eat it and not tell him?" Harmony asked as she picked up a can of meat.

"Sometimes." I hesitated. Could I trust her to keep a secret? "I change the numbers on the sheets so he doesn't know anything's gone."

"And he doesn't notice?"

I shook my head. There were times he didn't even notice *me*, let alone changed numbers on some sheet of paper. It wasn't that hard to take a can of meat.

"That means you could do it all the time," she said.

"I only do it when I need to."

Candy started barking again. Somebody was at the door or walking by the house—or my father was home. I'd lost track of time. I had to hope it was a stranger.

"Come on. We have to go upstairs right now."

I rushed across the basement, flipping the light off before Harmony had made it completely into the glow of the stairway light. We raced upstairs, and I flicked off the light and closed the basement door just as the front door opened.

"I'm home!" my father yelled.

I turned to Harmony. "It's my father. Please don't mention that I took you down to the basement."

She looked confused, but she nodded.

I went over to the stove, put the pot of potatoes on a burner and turned it on. Candy started yipping and yelping. She was happy to hear my father's voice. He always treated Candy well. I quickly let her out of the bathroom.

"Hello!" he called out from down the hall. I tried to judge his voice. He sounded happy, but not too happy. Maybe the elevator was halfway down— or halfway up—and this wouldn't be too bad.

"Don't take anything he says personal, okay?" I said to Harmony.

She nodded solemnly.

"That highway is usually so crowded and such a death trap, but somehow today the traffic wasn't nearly as—" My father stopped talking as he walked into the kitchen and saw Harmony.

"Dad, this is my friend Harmony."

"Hello," she said.

He looked at her intently, like he was trying to figure out a puzzle. "Harmony…like a symphony orchestra?"

"Something like that," she said.

"You know, I once had neighbors who had a dog named Harmony. Strange thing was, that dog couldn't sing a note to save her life."

He laughed at his joke—a sure sign that the elevator was heading up. Harmony gave a weak little smile.

"Not that I'm calling you a dog—"

"Harmony is in my class," I interjected. "We were here studying."

"Huh. I don't see any books out. Were you studying biology? You know, *sex education*?" He waggled his eyebrows.

"Harmony is my friend!" I snapped, trying to cut him off before he could say more or she could react to him.

"I'm just kidding around," he said with a frown. "You never seem to be able to take a joke."

"Oh, he can take a joke," Harmony said. "Robert is actually quite funny."

"Robert?"

"It *is* my name," I said.

Everybody at school had reacted to her calling me that, so why wouldn't he? A part of me wished she'd just call me Robbie. On the other hand, I liked that she didn't. I *was* Robert. It was my name. The name my parents—my mother— had given me.

"It certainly is. Perhaps I should call you Mr. Robert instead?"

"Robert will be fine," I said, ignoring his sarcasm. "The potatoes are on the stove. Harmony has to go now, and I'm going to walk her home."

"Are you going to carry her imaginary books as well?"

I didn't respond. "I'm going to walk Candy. I'll be back in twenty minutes."

I walked out of the room. I had the urge to grab Harmony and pull her along, but I knew if I did my father would make some comment about us holding hands. I called for Candy and she came.

She snarled and growled at Harmony. I clicked her leash onto her collar.

As soon as I closed the door behind us, Harmony spoke. "What is your dad's problem?"

"I don't know where to even start."

"I really wanted to ask him why he came home so early tonight," she said.

"You can't ever ask him that. Please. Don't."

"I wouldn't do that to you. *Never*," she said. "You know you don't have to walk me home."

"Yeah, I know, but I need to get away from him for a few minutes and Candy needed a walk," I explained. "It will also give me a chance to settle down, not feel so angry."

"You don't seem that angry."

"I am. Look, I'm sorry."

"You don't need to apologize for him. He really is a jerk, isn't he?"

"Sometimes. But some people really like him."

"Some people are stupid."

My father often had a girlfriend, although they never seemed to stick around for more than a month or two. Maybe they were stupid enough to date him but smart enough not to stay.

"At least he didn't hassle you about spending money on your new pants."

I laughed. "He didn't notice them."

"How could he not notice? They are spectacular pants."

"Just what I've always wanted. Spectacular pants. But believe me, I doubt he'd have noticed if I wasn't wearing *any* pants."

"Let's try to avoid testing that theory when I'm around," Harmony said.

We came up to her house—her foster home— and stopped.

"Are they treating you okay?" I asked.

"Yeah, they seem nice…surprisingly nice…but it could all be an act."

"So you're not thinking of running?"

"Not tonight. Besides, there's really no point. I'll wait it out. It won't be that long. My mother will probably get her act together in a couple of weeks—four or five max."

"Oh, that's right. Then you'll go home."

"Don't sound so disappointed."

It surprised me that I felt that way, and it surprised me even more that she'd heard it in my voice.

"There's always a fifty-fifty chance she'll screw things up. So it could be longer," she said.

"I know you've been in foster homes before, but exactly how many times?" I asked.

"More than I'd like to remember. Hey, I was just wondering...since you have a job and get paid, and you obviously don't spend it on clothing, what do you do with your money?"

I'd quickly learned that when Harmony didn't want to talk about something, she changed the subject. I recognized it because I used that trick myself.

"Well?" she asked.

"I'm saving up for a private jet."

"Seriously."

"I mean a yacht. I've always wanted a yacht."

"It's a car, right? You seem like the sort of guy who starts saving for a car years before they're old enough to drive. It's wheels, right?"

I just smiled and nodded.

"You don't seem like a gearhead, but guys are guys. Just out of curiosity, do *you* ever think about running away?"

"Why would I?" I asked.

"Come on, I've run away from places that are better than where you live."

"It's my home. It's my house. It's my place."

"Yeah, I guess I understand. There have been times when I should have called social services about my mother, but I didn't. I just stayed," she said.

She started up the walk to her house, and I called out to her. "What was its name?"

She turned and looked at me, confused by my question.

"Your polar bear, the one your mom took and sold." What was his name?

She smiled. "Polar. Polar the Bear. Stupid, right?"

"I like it. I would have called it the same thing," I said.

"Oh great, now I'm as hopeless as you."

"Or as cool. I'll see you tomorrow," I said. "Right?"

"You should come by my house, and we'll walk to school together. I'll even let you carry my imaginary books," she said with a wink. "Now you better get home and get to work. You haven't worked harder than me today."

I knew she was joking, but she was also right. I did have work to do tonight.

Then Harmony surprised me by coming back down the walk. What was she doing? When she was close enough, she threw her arms around my shoulders and gave me a big hug. My arms hung limply at my sides.

"See you tomorrow," she said and then turned and disappeared into her house.

I just stood there, too shocked to move. She'd hugged me. When was the last time anyone had hugged me? I couldn't remember. I'd just been hugged by some girl I hadn't even known existed until two days ago. A girl who only the day before had punched me in the nose. A girl who had just gone clothes shopping with me. A girl I'd told secrets that I'd never told anybody. A girl who most likely would be gone in a few days or at most a few weeks. Maybe that made it all okay.

# TEN

This was the eighth day in a row we had walked to school together. Harmony mostly talked and I mostly listened. And thought. Each morning I'd stop in front of her house and wait. The last three mornings her foster mother had stood at the door and given me a smile and a little wave. I'd waved back. Today Harmony had been a bit later than usual, so we weren't going to be as early as I liked to be. There was actually a danger we might be a minute or two late.

Neither of us had said it, but we tried to walk to school with just the two of us. If we saw somebody we knew—somebody I knew, for the most part—we'd slow down or speed up or take a slightly different route. Sometimes that didn't work, but most of the time it did. I was disappointed when it didn't. I thought she was too. Not that I'd admit it to anybody, but I felt like I didn't want to share her.

My friends were starting to bug me about me spending so much time with Harmony, and I heard some people thought we were a couple. I'd never been the subject of talk like that. I was the thin, tall kid who was smart and good at basketball. I wasn't the guy with the girlfriend. Not that she *was* my girlfriend.

Funny thing was, Harmony never ran out of things to say. The girl could talk. I was okay with that. Listening meant I was less likely to say anything that would reveal any more of my secrets. Even so, some of them came out.

Today Harmony was a little more feisty than usual. It made me uneasy. She was always close to the line. Two days earlier she'd yelled at a driver and given him the finger when we were crossing St. Clair. He'd pulled over, climbed out of his car and yelled at us, and we'd had to run away. Actually, I'd had to sort of drag her away because she wanted to get into it with him.

Today it looked like she was itching for a fight again. She'd been going on and on about some of the girls in our class. There was a group of girls— four or five, depending on if they were fighting with each other—who seemed to think they could control the school. They didn't bother me because I wasn't important enough for them to notice. It was almost impossible not to notice Harmony, though, and they weren't happy about her getting attention.

"If any of them even looks at me the wrong way today, I'm going to lose it on them," she said.

"No you're not. You're going to behave yourself today, right?"

"Depends. I'm nice to people who are nice to me. I bet none of those girls have ever been in a real fight in their entire lives," Harmony said.

"How about if we keep it that way? Just remember to use your words."

She laughed. "You're hilarious even when you don't mean to be."

"I'll take that as a compliment. Did you do your homework?"

"You're not my mother. Wait—my mother has never once asked me about my homework. Does your dad ever ask you about homework?"

"I don't need to be asked. Besides, he's too preoccupied with his own things."

"Is he still going up in the elevator?" she asked.

"He's pretty close to the top, I think."

I'd told her more and more about my father—more than I'd told anybody else. But there were so many things she didn't know, and I was never going to tell her. Still, it felt really good to have somebody to talk to. She could keep a secret. Besides, the fact that she would soon be going back to her mother and leaving the school meant she'd be taking my secrets away with her.

"I don't know if he slept much last night," I said.

"But he let you sleep?"

I nodded.

"Your father is such a jerk. Not that my mother isn't a jerk too. Do you know how many times she's been to rehab?"

I shook my head.

"Four—no, five times."

"And you had to go to a foster home each time?"

"Not the first couple of times. My nana took care of me."

"Your grandmother?"

"Yeah, my mother's mother. She practically raised me. We lived with her until I was nine, and then, well, you know, she passed."

*Passed.* A polite word for *died.*

"That was four, almost five years ago. I still really miss her."

"My grandmother and grandfather used to live with us."

"And your father drove them away?" she asked.

"They died. My grandfather a year after my mother and then my grandmother six months after that."

"Wow, three family members before you were even six years old. You should be more screwed up than you are."

"Thanks, I guess."

We walked for a bit without talking. That always happened when one of us had said too much.

"Do you know what's not fair?" Harmony finally asked, breaking the silence.

"That people die?"

"That the *wrong* people always die."

I couldn't help but laugh, though nothing she said was meant to be funny.

"My nana, who really loved me, died and my mother, who didn't care for me, lived. Does it sound mean for me to think that about my mother?"

I shook my head. "I've thought it too...about my mother dying and my father living."

"It's okay to think that," she said. "Right?"

I didn't know if it was right or wrong, I just knew it was how I felt and, apparently, how she felt too. We kept walking and stopped talking again. I wondered if we'd say another word the rest of the way.

"Wanna trade lunches?" Harmony asked. This was a safe thing to talk about.

"I was hoping you'd ask."

She pulled out a banana and half a sandwich from her lunch bag as we walked. Trading had become part of our morning routine so we wouldn't have to do it at lunch. The guys had noticed I was eating something other than jam sandwiches and knew what we were doing, but nobody said anything anymore.

I took the items she gave me, put them in my bag and started to remove the half sandwich I'd wrapped separately.

"Let me guess. It's a jam sandwich," she said.

"You could have a future working for the psychic hotline."

"First off, I knew you were going to say that, and second, couldn't you bring something else for lunch instead? I know for a fact that you have peanut butter in your basement food hoard."

"I really don't like peanut butter."

"If you're going to trade it to me anyway, what does it matter?" she asked.

"I didn't know you like peanut butter."

"After all this jam, I'm pretty well ready for dog food on a cracker."

"We do have crackers and dog food. I can arrange that."

"How about peanut butter tomorrow?"

"You don't have to trade lunches with me," I said.

"Yes, I do, but I'm afraid that if you fatten up, you won't fit into your fancy new pants."

"Maybe you could convince Mrs. Levy to let out the waist."

We stopped at St. Clair and waited for the cars to clear. There were traffic signals half a block away, but we never went that far. There was a gap coming up.

"Let's go!"

I ran across the four car lanes and two sets of streetcar tracks, but Harmony took her time. She always did that. It was like she was forcing the cars to slow down—or daring them to hit her. One car blared its horn and sped past, just barely missing her.

She joined me on the curb.

"Are you trying to get hit?"

"It missed me."

Harmony turned to the left and started walking.

"I figured you knew the way by now," I said.

"If we head down this alley, we can go through the back gate into the schoolyard. It's shorter."

She was right, but there were reasons not to take this route.

"Are you scared of the alley?" she asked.

"No." Okay, that was a lie. Most of us avoided this alley.

"It's eight fifteen in the morning. Bad things happen at night." I saw a twinkle in her eyes. "I'm going through the alley. Are you coming?"

If I didn't go, I'd never hear the end of it. Besides, I didn't think it was smart for her to go alone. I also thought she might be right, that it would probably be safe in the daytime.

We turned into the alley. It was deserted. Closed garage doors and garbage cans lined the lane. There were no cars or people to be seen.

"See? There's nothing to worry about," Harmony said. "So stop worr—"

Three guys came out from between two garages farther down the alley. They were older, bigger and louder than us, and they outnumbered us. My instincts were to turn and run but I doubted

Harmony was going to run and there was no way I was leaving her behind.

They got closer and louder. I tried not to make eye contact. I thought if I just stared straight ahead, not looking at them, they wouldn't look at me. We had almost passed them when one of them reached out, grabbed me by the arm and spun me around. It was like an electric shock went through my entire body.

"Where do you think you're going?" he demanded.

I was too stunned and scared to speak.

Harmony jumped in. "We're going to school. Maybe you should do the same thing, because you have a lot of things to learn."

The second guy reached out and grabbed her bag, snatching it from her shoulder. She tried to react, but the third one grabbed her from behind, pinning her arms. She struggled to get free.

"Leave her alone!" I yelled. I was trying to break free too, but the first guy held me tighter and swung me around until we were face-to-face.

"You got anything else you want to say?"

I didn't answer. I looked down at the ground, but my fingers balled into fists.

The guy holding me grabbed my bag and tossed it to the guy who had Harmony's pack. He opened up Harmony's bag and started grabbing things and dropping them to the ground. An apple, half a jam sandwich, a book. He turned her backpack upside down, and the rest of her lunch and a couple more books tumbled out. He shook the bag again, making sure it was empty, and then dropped it on the ground as well.

"Nothing," he said.

"Do either of you have money?" the first guy asked me.

I shook my head. I was so scared I felt like I wasn't even in my body anymore. What were they going to do to us? There was nobody around…

"I have some money," Harmony said. "Let me go, and I'll get it out."

The guy released her, and she started digging in her pockets.

"Here," Harmony said.

She was holding a twenty-dollar bill in her hand. Then she dropped it, and it fluttered to the ground. As the guy bent down to get it, she brought her knee up, and it connected to his face with a sickening thud. He groaned and staggered, almost toppling over.

Fast as lightning, she grabbed the lid of a metal garbage can beside her and hit him again on the top of his head. He crumpled to the ground.

I was desperately shaking my arm to get loose from the guy holding me, and I accidentally hit him in the face with my elbow. I heard a loud *snap*, and his nose exploded. The blood spurted out, and he released me, clutching his nose. He fell to his knees.

The third guy just stood there, staring at us. He looked as stunned, shocked and surprised as I felt.

Harmony started swinging the garbage lid, wielding it like Wonder Woman. The guy stepped back, tripped, almost fell over my bag on the ground, regained his balance and then turned and ran down the alley in the direction we'd just come from. Harmony threw the lid frisbee style in his direction. It clattered on the pavement.

"Come on!" she yelled.

She grabbed her books, backpack and the twenty-dollar bill, then started running. I picked up my pack and ran too, quickly catching up to her.

Harmony reached out and grabbed my free hand, and we kept running. I kept checking over my shoulder to see if the guys were chasing us, but two were still on the ground and the third had vanished. We rounded the corner at the end of the alley and kept running, right through the open gate of the schoolyard. I was relieved to see a teacher outside on duty and the yard filled with people waiting for the bell. We were safe.

We came to a stop at the base of a tree. I looked around and saw that people had turned in our direction. Maybe it was because we were running, or maybe it was the dazed look in our eyes, or… we were still holding hands. We both realized it at the same time, and we released our grip.

"Are you okay?" I asked.

She shrugged. "You?"

"It was like watching a movie starring Disharmony, super ninja warrior."

She started to laugh, but it was a strange laugh—like she wasn't laughing as much as trying not to cry.

"I think I have to sit down," she said.

She slumped against the tree trunk, and I sat down beside her.

"Where did you ever learn to use the lid of a garbage can as a weapon?"

"Doesn't everybody do that?" she asked.

"Only Captain America, Wonder Woman and now you."

"You use what you've got. I've learned that. You did pretty good with those pointy elbows of yours."

"I think I might have broken his nose."

"I hope you did! He deserved it."

"Should we tell the principal? You know, have him call the police?" I asked.

"And tell them you broke somebody's nose and I put my knee into a guy's face and then hit him with a garbage-can lid?"

I now realized that both of us were shaking.

"I thought they were going to do to us what we did to them," I said.

"So did I. You ever been beaten up before?" Harmony asked.

"Other than by you?"

She started laughing again. "You really do make me laugh, Robert."

"Just what I want, girls laughing at me," I said before adding, "Yeah, I've lost some fights."

"I can't picture that."

"You can't picture me losing?" I asked.

"I can't picture you fighting."

"I don't. Not now. Not anymore."

"But you did?"

"Before—a few years ago."

"And now you don't fight?" she asked.

"No."

"Because you were beaten up a lot?"

I didn't answer. That wasn't the reason, but I couldn't tell her what was.

"I've been beaten up," she said.

"I didn't know superheroes got beat up."

This time she didn't laugh.

"I'm sorry. I didn't know," I said.

"It's happened a few times."

"Is that why your mother went to jail?" I asked.

"Not my mother. It was two of the assorted loser boyfriends she's brought around over the years, and one of them did go to jail for hitting me."

I felt a rush of anger. What sort of jerk beats up a kid?

"I'm glad it wasn't your mother."

"She didn't hit me, but she didn't stop them. That's not much better. Your father ever hit you?"

"Never."

"Never?"

"Not once." I paused. Time for more secrets. "He'd have to notice me to hit me."

She slid her hand over and took my hand. She did it gently and subtly, so that even somebody standing right there probably wouldn't have seen it. "I notice you."

I wanted to say something, but I didn't know what to say. The bell rang. Harmony went to get up, and I kept holding her hand. "Not yet," I said. She slumped back down.

It would take a few minutes for everybody to line up and the lines to start moving into the school. I just wanted to sit with her a little longer. It was nice to be noticed.

# ELEVEN

We joined a bunch of students, including Taylor, for the walk home. Safety in numbers. Harmony said we should take a shortcut through the alley, and I looked at her like she was insane. She said she was only kidding. She sure had a weird sense of humor. We stuck to the streets.

The whole school seemed to know what had happened in the alley that morning. Harmony had told the story at lunch, and it had spread like lightning. It was strange hearing her tell it. She'd added some extra details. Somehow, between the alley in the morning and lunch in the cafeteria, the three guys had gotten older and bigger and scarier.

She had also made it seem like I had played a bigger, braver part and that my clocking the guy in the nose hadn't been accidental. It felt good to be a hero, even if it was more in the story than in the alley. I had to hand it to Harmony, she could really tell a story.

Sal—who has known me the longest—said something about how I used to get into fights all the time. Harmony looked surprised, though I'd already told her that. The others looked just as surprised. Fighting wasn't what I was known for. At least, not now.

By the end of the day I'd had lots of people saying things to me, some offering congratulations. There was also something different about the way people were looking at me—they were even acting differently. I was being noticed. That was both comforting and uncomforting.

Why was so much of life like that—good and bad, hot and cold, up and down, in and out? Why couldn't anything just be one way or the other? Why did things always have to be so complicated?

One by one the pack broke off until it was just Harmony and me left. There was no longer any safety in numbers. My antennae went up, and she quickly noticed.

"Those losers are probably still in the hospital."

"Do you really think so?" I asked.

"Don't be stupid. Of course not, but that doesn't mean they're going to be here. Had you ever seen any of them before?"

"Never."

"Then you'll probably never see them again," she said.

"No harm in being careful."

"Do you want me to walk *you* home?"

"Funny. I'm probably better off without you. I'm faster than you, so I can run away from danger."

"Then why didn't you run from danger in the alley?" she asked.

"I wasn't going anywhere without you. Besides, he'd already grabbed me."

"Yeah, but if he hadn't, if you could have run away, would you have left me there?" she asked.

"I would never have left you."

We were both silent for a moment. "I guess I owe you an apology," she said finally.

"Wait, you're apologizing and I don't have a witness? Nobody will ever believe it happened."

"Can you shut up for a minute? Look, I was wrong. We shouldn't have gone down that alley. I should have listened to you."

"Maybe you will next time," I suggested.

"No promises. If you don't make promises, you don't have to break them." Harmony hesitated. "Sort of like if you don't pray for anything, you don't have to worry about being disappointed."

She knew me too well.

"Do you work tonight?" she asked as we approached her house.

"Yeah, from four thirty to closing at nine." I gestured toward the house. "Are they still treating you well?"

"They're really nice. This is probably the nicest place I've ever been."

"That's great. But as soon as your mother gets her act together, you'll be going back home, right?"

"Of course," she said. "Would you like to meet her?"

"Your mother?"

"Don't be stupid. I mean Darlene, my foster mother. She's been asking to meet you. She said you can come over for dinner one night. And before you say no, because that's what you do, aren't you at least a little curious to see what a foster home is like?"

Harmony was right about both things. She had learned that my first answer to anything new was no. What she didn't know was that I was more than just curious. I'd actually had the strange thought of wondering if my father died, could I live at this foster home and stay right here in the neighborhood? Maybe it would be good to go in and see the place for myself.

"I'd like to meet her but not today," I said. "Can I ask you a question?"

"Yeah, of course."

"You keep ending up in foster care, and this one you think is the very best. So I'm just wondering…" I let the sentence trail off.

"Why do I want to go back to my mother?" she asked.

I nodded.

"For the exact same reason that you don't come into foster care."

"What?"

"I've never been in a foster home where they don't give me food and put clothes on me. I've never been in one where they just go out and leave me alone at night. I've never been in one where I get ignored and they don't even notice I live there. So the real question is, why do you stay with your father?"

"It's my house. He's my father. He needs me."

"And that's my answer. It's my home. She's my mother. She needs me. Now do you understand?"

"I guess so, but…it's just you deserve better than that."

"And you don't?" she asked.

*Did* I deserve better?

"I have to go or I'll be late for work," I said quickly and then turned and walked away. I knew the answer to her question. Even though I hadn't answered, I knew. I already had what I deserved. Somehow all of this was my fault.

# TWELVE

Mrs. Watson—she had asked me to call her Darlene—had a snack waiting for us. It had taken three more days of Harmony hounding me on the walk home before I'd agreed to go in. Giving in was the only way to get her to stop asking.

Mrs. Watson seemed very nice and made me feel welcome, but I was still a little anxious. I tried to chew with my mouth closed and keep my elbows off the table. It had a tablecloth on it, and there was a bowl of fruit in the middle. There were nice pictures on the walls and nice furniture. Everything was nice. The place was clean and tidy. It even smelled clean and tidy. Everything about it seemed so normal. Not normal like my house but normal like my friends' places, and filled with normal things. Including the food. Food was normal. Rows of cans hidden in the basement wasn't. This foster home wouldn't be the worst place to end up.

Mrs. Watson poured me a second glass of lemonade without even asking if I wanted one.

"Thank you," I said.

She was older, smiley and very friendly. Harmony had told me that Darlene and her husband had three kids—two were married and the youngest was away at trade school. Her husband, Frank, was an electrician.

"Are you sure you don't want another cookie or two?" she asked.

"Before he says no, he actually does want some more," Harmony said. She grabbed three more off the plate Mrs. Watson was holding out and put them on my plate.

"Thank you."

"Such good manners," Mrs. Watson said. "That's a sign your father raised you right."

It was also a sign that Harmony had told her about my having a father but no mother. Otherwise she would have said *parents*.

"It's just so wonderful to have Harmony bring home her, um, *friend*."

I could tell by the way she said it that she was wondering if it should be *boyfriend*. Most of the kids at school thought that as well. I worked hard not to think about it. Neither Harmony nor I said anything, and there was silence in the room—which Mrs. Watson quickly broke.

"Harmony talks about you *all* the time."

I looked over at Harmony. Was she blushing?

"I already know you're the smartest, most serious student in the class, you work part-time at the Priamos' butcher shop and you're a basketball star."

"We just lost the first game of the season, so not so much a star," I said.

"He got a double-double," Harmony said. "Robert did his part."

"We still lost."

"And modest too," said Mrs. Watson. "Does your father ever go to see you play?"

"Uh…his work is on the other side of the city, so he can't get there on time to watch."

Even if he worked near the school, he probably wouldn't come. I wouldn't have wanted him to be there anyway.

"He must be very proud of you," Mrs. Watson said.

I hadn't even bothered to tell him I was on the team. If I had, one of two things would have happened, neither of them good. Either he wouldn't have cared at all or he would have cared too much. Caring too much would have been worse. It would have meant that no matter what I or the team did, it wouldn't be good enough.

"We're so happy that Harmony has become the team manager. I told her I want to come to a game to watch, but she won't let me," Mrs. Watson said.

"What would you do, clap when I hand out a towel?"

"I could do that. We are just so happy to have you with us. You're a delight to have around."

I chuckled slightly.

"What? Don't you think I'm a delight?" Harmony asked, eyes blazing.

I held up my arms in surrender. "*Delight* is the exact word I use to describe you when I talk about you to other people."

"You talk about me to other people?" she asked.

"You're all I ever talk about," I said. "I stop strangers to talk about you. When I walk Candy, I talk to other dogs about you. When I—"

"Shut right up," she said.

I didn't talk to people about her, but I did *think* about her. A lot. A whole lot.

"Although I'm sure those boys in the alley didn't think either of you was so delightful," Mrs. Watson said.

I was surprised Harmony had told Mrs. Watson about that. I certainly hadn't told my father.

"I'm glad you were there to protect Harmony."

"I think it was more like us protecting each other." I looked at my watch. "I have to get going."

"Are you sure you won't stay for supper?"

"Thank you, but I've got to get going." To make supper and walk Candy and start studying.

"Another time then," Mrs. Watson said.

"Thank you. Definitely."

We all got to our feet, and Mrs. Watson gave me a hug. It felt awkward. Harmony stood off to the side and smirked.

"See you tomorrow," Harmony said.

I'd made supper. And then I waited and tried to keep it warm. The clock kept ticking. I waited some more. And he didn't come. I stood at the front window and counted cars, figuring the next set of lights coming down the road would be his. But it wasn't. Then I started bargaining—first with myself and then with God. Bargaining seemed different than praying. And then I thought of Harmony doing the same. If she were here, she'd know I was doing that. Okay, if my father's wasn't the next car, it would be one of the next ten or twenty. But still it wasn't.

Then I stopped bargaining and ate dinner. I pulled out my math homework and did questions between bites. It helped to get my mind off worrying about where my father might be.

Three or four times, Candy started barking and I went to the front window and looked out. It was just a passing car or somebody walking by. A couple of times I went to the TV and turned on the twenty-four-hour news channel to see if there had been a bad accident on the 401—his route home. Nothing there. That was both reassuring and troubling. If he'd been caught in a massive traffic jam that had blocked the whole highway, he wouldn't be able to let me know what had happened because he didn't have a cell phone. But then I started thinking, What if he hadn't been caught *behind* an accident but had been *in* an accident, a bad accident? What if I saw our car on TV, and it was all smashed in? Or there was a knock on the door and a police officer was standing there, telling me my father was dead?

I'd gone down to the basement. I'd needed to see all the food on the shelves. I'd known it would be there, but it had made me feel better to look at it. I had taken a can of meat. Nothing fancy, just a can of Spam. I'd adjusted the tally sheets so it wouldn't be missed. I'd opened it up, eaten half and given the

other half to Candy. She deserved it. She was here
for supper. She was here for me.

I wrapped up my father's dinner and put it
in the fridge. Then I did the dishes. Somewhere
between washing and drying them, it went from
dark to real dark outside.

I needed to create order. I put my math text-
book and finished homework in my pack. I made
a sandwich—one half jam and one half peanut
butter—and put it and an apple in the fridge.

For the second time, I walked around the house
to make sure all the windows were closed and the
doors were locked. I paused at the front window
and peered up the street. Deserted. No motion.
No headlights. The lights were off at most of the
houses, and people were turning in for the night.
I wished I could turn in.

If he was going to be late, he should have called
and let me know. He could have used a pay phone.
If he still had a cell phone, I could have called him.
Then again, he'd had a cell phone the time he was
gone for days and days. I'd kept calling him, and
he'd kept not answering it.

I picked up the remote. It was almost time for
the eleven o'clock news. Maybe I could find out
something. I was about to sit down when the phone
rang. I ran across the room, my feet barely touching
the floor. Was it him calling or somebody calling
about him or—

"Hello!" I practically yelled into the phone.

There was dead air and then, "Hi, Robert."

My heart sank and rose at the same time. It was
Harmony. More than once I'd thought about calling
her tonight—not to tell her he wasn't here but to
hear her voice.

"Hey, Harmony," I said, trying to sound casual,
like nothing was wrong.

"I'm sorry for calling so late, but I had to wait
until everybody here was asleep." Her voice was
very quiet, like she was trying hard not to wake
anyone up.

"I hope your father won't give you a hard time
about me calling you this late."

"He won't even notice." That was true.

"I didn't wake you up, did I?"

"No, I won't be going to bed for a while."

"I figured you'd still be up, working longer than anybody else," she said. "Right?"

"Right."

"I just needed to talk to you," she said.

There was something about her voice. Had she been crying?

"Did something happen? Are you all right?" I asked.

There was only silence at her end.

"Harmony, you didn't call this late just to say hello or see if I was studying, so tell me what's wrong."

She sniffled. She *had* been crying—she *still* was crying.

"Tell me what's wrong."

There was more dead air. For a second I thought she'd hung up.

"They can't find her," she said finally.

"Find who?"

"My mother. My social worker called to tell Darlene, to tell me. She left rehab...and she's gone...again."

"I'm sorry." I *was* sorry, but another part of me was happy, because it meant Harmony would be staying around longer. I felt bad, disloyal, for even thinking that way.

"I just feel so...so...I don't know, like nobody cares for me. My own mother doesn't care for me. I'm so alone."

"I understand," I said.

"I knew you would."

She had no idea how much I understood. I had the urge to tell her about my father not coming home, but she didn't need that right now. Even if I wasn't sure what I *should* say to her, I knew what I *shouldn't* say.

"You need to go to bed," I finally said. "Go to sleep, and it might be better tomorrow."

"Do you really think so?"

"How can it be worse?" I asked.

"You should try to get to sleep too. And thanks."

"For what?"

"For making me feel like I'm not alone. Good night."

"Good night. I'll be there early tomorrow to get you because of basketball practice."

"I'll be ready. Good night, Robert."

I hung up the phone. Now I just had to do the same thing, believe the same thing I'd told Harmony. Tomorrow everything *would* be all right.

"Candy, come."

I took her out to do her business, then checked the doors and windows one last time. Then we went up to my room, and I closed the door, put a chair against it and got into bed. Tomorrow would be better. It had to be.

~~1,615~~ 1,614

# THIRTEEN

I had the notebook open to the first page and the first number—5,012. Then I flipped through to the last entry page. I crossed out *1,615* and wrote down *1,614*. That was a better number—a smaller number.

Candy gave a little yip, and I looked down. She wagged her tail, and I gave her a scratch behind the ear.

"It's going to be all right." I squatted and wrapped my arms around her neck. I gave her a big squeeze. Bigger than usual.

"You mean a lot to me, girl. You know I'll always be here to take care of you. I'll be back right after school, and no matter what, you're going to be okay." I paused. "I have a plan, and it includes you."

I released my grip and stood up. She pressed against my leg, clearly not wanting me to leave. I didn't want to go either, but I had no choice. I had to keep doing what needed to be done. I'd fallen asleep around three and slept right through until just before my alarm. Before three, I'd lain there awake, listening for the sound of my father's car pulling up and going over my plans. I didn't just have *a* plan—I had *plans*. Plan A, plan B and now a new one—plan C. Lying there in bed, unable to sleep, I'd gone over the items needed for each plan to make sure I could execute whichever one I needed to.

I went downstairs, grabbed my pack and slipped out the door. I pulled it closed behind me. I took two steps across the porch and then spun around and tried the door. It was locked. This morning it seemed more important than ever to check.

I did a half jog to Harmony's place. I wasn't in danger of being late for practice, but I wanted to have a bit more time with Harmony—walk to school a bit slower than usual so she would have a chance to talk, if she wanted to. I just hoped she was ready to leave when I got there.

As I jogged, I thought about my father. I'd considered calling his work to see if he had gone straight there from wherever he was. But then I thought he might have called in himself and given them some story about being sick. If I called now, they'd know he had lied. Him getting fired because of me would be so much worse than if he got found out some other way.

Before going to bed, I'd thought of calling Uncle Jack and Aunt Cora—just to talk. My aunt was always nice, and Uncle Jack was, well, just a good guy. I knew I couldn't though—how would I explain calling so late? I didn't want to bother them, and I wasn't going to tell them my father hadn't come home. I used to drop in on them after school—they didn't live that far away. But I'd stopped doing that because my father had told me it was rude and I shouldn't bug them. I missed them. Even more, I wished they missed me too. So really, what would have been the point in calling them? I knew they couldn't fix this.

Anyway, I kept telling myself, being alone wasn't that big a deal anyway. It wasn't like my father did much for me even when he was home. What was another day or two, or a week or two? I'd survive. I had plans. No matter what happened.

I turned the corner and was surprised to see Harmony waiting for me outside her house. She never waited outside. This was different. Different made me nervous.

"How are you doing?" I called out.

She didn't answer but got to her feet and started walking. I scrambled to catch up.

"Seriously, are you all right?" I asked.

"It's not like she hasn't pulled this sort of thing before," Harmony said.

"Do you want to talk about it?"

"There's nothing to talk about. You sure you didn't get into trouble for my calling so late?"

She'd given me an opening, but I wasn't taking it. "No trouble at all." Nobody could know he'd done this to me. Not even her. Maybe especially her.

It was strange, but his taking off felt a lot like my mother being dead—I didn't want people to know about it because I felt like somehow it was my fault. I knew it was stupid, but that didn't stop me from feeling it.

"So do you know anything else about your mother?" I asked.

"No. Maybe I'll know more by the end of the day."

When we reached the spot where we usually tried to cross St. Clair, she walked right onto the road without waiting for a gap in traffic. One car swerved around her and another driver honked at her. She spun around and yelled at him. A couple more cars and a big truck slowed almost to a stop. She gave them the evil eye and even slowed her walk. But she reached the sidewalk on the other side safely. I waited for an opening and then ran across.

"Are you crazy?" I asked as I joined her.

"If you act like you own the road, they'll stop. Stop being such a suck."

"A *suck*? I'm a suck because I don't want to get hit by a car?"

"You're a suck for a whole lot of reasons."

I stood there in shock. What was up with her? Then Harmony turned toward the alley. I grabbed her arm and spun her around.

"There's no way we're going down that alley this morning. I won't let you."

She looked me squarely in the eyes. "First, do you remember what happened the first time you grabbed me by the arm?"

Instantly I let go of her.

"And second, *let* me? Since when do you think you're in charge of me?"

"I'm not…I'm sorry. Please, can we not go down that alley? You know what could happen."

"And if I decide to go that way, what are you going to do about it?" she asked.

I took a deep breath. "I wouldn't want to, but I'd go with you."

"Really?" she asked.

"Really."

"I take back the suck part. You're actually *stupid*." Again I was shocked. But she kept talking. "I'm not going down the alley because I'm not going to school."

"What are you talking about?"

"I'm going to find my mother."

She started walking away. I followed her.

"You can't do that!"

"I can do what I want. I'll get on the streetcar and then the subway, and I'll check out some places she might be."

"But you'll miss basketball practice and school. They'll call your foster home and then you'll get in trouble and—"

"I don't care," she said and started walking again.

I ran after her again. This time I got in front of her and stopped, making sure not to touch her. "Even if you don't care, *I* care. I don't want you to get in trouble. You could get suspended. Or what if the Watsons decide you're causing too much trouble and don't want to keep you any longer?"

"What's the worst that can happen? They ship me to another place?"

"You said it was the best place you've been, so why risk losing it?"

"I don't have a choice. I need to do *something*."

"What if I go with you?" I asked.

"You'd cut school?"

I couldn't do that. "What if I went with you right *after* school?"

"How is that better?" she asked.

"First off, we won't miss school or basketball, so we won't get in trouble. We'll borrow somebody's phone, and you can call Mrs. Watson and ask if you can eat at my place because we have to study for a big test. Then we can go without anybody knowing, and you won't get in trouble."

"And we'll call your father and tell him you're at my place," she said.

"Yeah," I said, though I knew it wouldn't be necessary. He might not be home tonight anyway. "So do we have a deal?"

Harmony looked skeptical. "And you'll really go with me after school?"

"I will."

"And you're not just saying this thinking you can talk me out of it?"

"I can never talk you out of anything. Look, I just don't want you to get in trouble. I don't want you to have to leave the Watsons' or change schools. So…deal?"

"Fine. Let's go to school," she said.

Our last class of the day was English. I liked English. And I liked Ms. Gay, our teacher. What I didn't like was that in forty minutes Harmony and I were going to travel across the city, probably into a bad situation. Even if nobody found out what we did, this still had the potential to get us into real trouble.

Ms. Gay handed back our last assignment. She made comments to students as she gave them their paper. Each comment was kind, even if the mark wasn't necessarily that good. I wasn't worried about my mark—at least, not too worried.

Ms. Gay stopped beside my desk. "I think you outdid yourself," she said as she placed my paper on my desk. I saw the mark—a very big red A+. "Outstanding. I really think you could be a writer when you grow up."

"Thanks." It was a nice thing to say, but really, could you make a living that way? I wasn't sure what I was going to do, but it certainly wasn't going to be writing. I was going to do something that made money. Maybe a teacher. Or a lawyer. Lawyers on TV always seemed to drive nice cars and live in big houses. And it was guaranteed that they had good food and wore nice clothes, and I was sure their children didn't have to worry about what was coming next. That was important to me. I didn't want my kids to have to live being worried. I wanted something better for them.

Ms. Gay continued along the row, and Harmony leaned over to talk to me. "Big shock," she whispered. "You getting a good mark."

"How did you do?"

She turned the paper so I could see the grade. "A solid B—just what I aim for."

I wanted to ask her why she didn't aim for an A when Ms. Gay, who had finished handing out the papers, started to talk.

"Today we're going to do a fun little exercise. I want each of you to write a few paragraphs about an object or thing that you think best represents you."

She smiled and looked around the class, and her smile faded. "And judging from your expressions,

you either don't understand the assignment or
think I'm a bit crazy for even suggesting it. Which
is it? Robert?"

A few of my friends and a couple of the teachers
had picked up on Harmony using my full name,
and I was Robert to them now too. I didn't mind.
I just wished Ms. Gay hadn't singled me out.

"Um, I think we just need a little more expla-
nation," I suggested, although it *did* sound pretty
weird.

"Okay. Maybe you can think of yourself as an
eagle because you fly high, or as a transport truck
because you always deliver, or as a pen because you
have so much you want to say," she said.

"Or a pig because you eat such big lunches,"
Taylor called out from the back. Everybody
laughed.

"Let's stick with positives," Ms. Gay said. "Your
best feature. Okay, start thinking!"

This was a stupid assignment, but what choice
did I have? At least it would stop me from thinking
about my father being gone, and about me and
Harmony taking off to try to find her mother.

Ms. Gay had mentioned an eagle, but I was no eagle. I had another idea.

*

Ms. Gay gathered up the assignments. She looked at the papers as she collected them. The ones I could see had only a few lines or so on them. I knew Harmony hadn't written anything except her name. I'd put down enough to fill almost the entire page.

I had written about how I was like a cheetah. I moved fast, I was thin, and I had to be smart to survive. What I hadn't written was that cheetahs were solitary and didn't live in a family. I didn't write that even when my father was there, I was living alone. That's what I really wanted to write. I wanted to tell her I had been left all alone the night before. But, of course, I didn't.

"Well," Ms. Gay began as she stood at the front of the class, "judging by the lack of content on these pages, it's clear that that assignment was a real miss."

She dropped the papers into the garbage can beside her desk. I was shocked.

"I was trying to be too cute," Ms. Gay said. "All I wanted was for you to write about yourselves. That's what tomorrow's assignment will be—to write about who you are, what you're about, what you believe in, what you like, what you hope to become. Does that work better?"

Before anybody could answer, the bell rang. The day was over. At least, the school day was over. What was still to happen to Harmony and me was just the beginning. I wished I knew what the ending was going to be.

# FOURTEEN

We walked a few blocks with the guys, then told them that Harmony needed to do some shopping and I was going along to help carry her bags. Of course, that made me the butt of numerous jokes about holding her purse—she didn't even have one—and being her fashion consultant. I didn't care what they had to say. It was part of our cover. We walked an extra five blocks along St. Clair before getting on the streetcar because I didn't want anybody we knew seeing us get on.

I'd thought of a whole lot of ways I could try to persuade Harmony not to go, but I didn't use any of them. All I could really hope was that my being with her would make this search safer for her. I also had to hope we'd be home before it got too late.

It wasn't going to be an issue for me no matter how late it was, but if Harmony wasn't home by about nine, she'd get into trouble.

I had enough money with me for the round-trip fare. Harmony had brought along enough for her fare and for supper. I'd asked Sal to go and let Candy out into the backyard. He was one of the few people Candy didn't hate. She didn't like him, but she didn't bite him. That was about as good as it got. Harmony was now in the same category as Sal. She'd been around enough that Candy had gotten used to her. Sal knew where I'd hidden a spare key. I could trust him with that too, and it wasn't like I trusted many people.

Harmony and I settled into seats at the back of the streetcar.

"Where exactly are we going?" I asked.

"The East End, where I'm from."

"If you lived in the East End, why did they put you in a foster home in the West End?"

"They probably figure the farther away they send me, the less likely it is I'll run away."

"But if they kept you closer, wouldn't you be less likely to run?"

"Maybe they should make you my social worker."

"I'm not that brave. And besides, so far it's worked. You're still here." Then I had another thought. "You *are* coming back with me, right? You're not running away?"

"I'm not running anywhere." She hesitated. "Not tonight anyway."

"How many times have you run away before?"

"A lot."

"And what happens?"

"Sometimes they find me. Sometimes the police bring me back. Sometimes I just get cold and hungry and come back on my own. You know, this is the longest I've ever been in a foster home without taking off for at least a night."

"I guess it's a good home and they're good people," I said.

"And I guess you have something to do with it. If I ran away, who'd take care of you? It's not like your father does."

She didn't know how right she was right now.

"I'm pretty good at taking care of myself," I answered.

"That doesn't make it right. We're kids. Aren't the parents supposed to be there for the kids?"

"I'll always be there for my kids."

She chuckled. "You have kids I don't know about?"

"I just mean I'll do the right thing for my kids, for my family, for my wife."

"So you also have a wife? Should I be jealous?"

"Maybe she should be jealous of you. Look, I just want to be a good parent," I said.

"If it were any other kid talking about being a good parent, it would just sound stupid," she said.

"And with me it doesn't?"

"Half the time you sound like you're already an adult."

Somebody in my house had to be an adult.

"You're going to be a great parent," she said.

"I'm going to try."

"You'll do it. You've had a role model for how to become a good parent," she said.

"You think my father is a role model?"

"A bad role model is still a role model. You learn what you shouldn't do, and that lets you know what you should do."

She was right. I'd learned a lot from my father. I was never going to be like him.

We rode along in silence. There were a couple of stops, and people got on and off the streetcar.

"You know you could do worse," Harmony said.

"Worse than what?"

"Worse than having me as a wife."

"If you're going to propose, shouldn't you get down on one knee?"

"Shut right up. I'm not proposing. I'm never, *ever* getting married."

I knew that someday I was going to find somebody to marry me, and I was going to treat her right. I'd treat her so well that she'd never want to leave.

"I'm just saying that you'd be pretty lucky to end up with somebody *like* me," she said.

"You could do worse too…you know, than having me as a husband."

"Boy, somebody has an inflated view of himself."

"You don't think I'd be a good husband?"

She shrugged. "You'd be better than most of the jokers at our school, but that's setting the bar pretty low. You know, a couple of the girls in our class really like you."

"Only a couple?"

She laughed.

"Do I get names?"

"You can figure it out. You're a smart guy." She paused. "You really are a smart guy, aren't you?"

"I don't have much choice. I guess neither do you."

"We have to be smart enough to take care of ourselves. Being scared can make you smart," she said.

If that were the case, I must be the smartest person in the world. Again I considered telling her about my father not coming home the night before, but I didn't. I couldn't. I felt a wave of shame. He didn't care enough about me to even come home and make sure I was okay. He might not come home tonight or the night after or the night after.

I just didn't want Harmony to know that. Besides, this mission wasn't about me. It was about her.

"Do you know why I don't have many friends?" Harmony asked.

"You're still new to the school."

"That isn't it."

"Is it because you're obnoxious?" I asked.

"Ha. That's not it either. You know you're really my only friend."

"What about the guys?" I asked.

She laughed. "They're not even *your* friends."

"What?

"They're just people you're friendly with, but that doesn't make them your friends."

"What are you talking about? Sal's, like, my best friend since second grade."

"If he's your best friend, why do I know more about you than the guy you've known for years?"

I was going to argue, but she was right. I'd already told her things Sal didn't know. That nobody else knew.

"You're different," she said.

"You're different too," I said.

"I'm not different, I'm just angry. I'm angry all the time. You, you're really different. I don't know why, but you are."

She was right—I was different. Different from my friends, my father and even her. I'd known that for a long time. I just hadn't thought anybody else could see it.

It felt like we'd both said too much, so we rode along in silence for a while.

"I was wondering, where are we going to look for your mother?"

"She has a few places, a few bars, that she likes. We'll start with one and then move on to the next."

"But if you know about these places, why didn't you just tell your social worker, and she could have looked or asked the people at the rehab place to look?"

"It doesn't work that way. If she leaves, they let her leave. My grandmother used to say, 'You can lead a horse to water, but you can't make it drink.' Do you know what that means?"

"Sure. You can't force people to do something they don't want to do."

"I figured you'd know that one too." Suddenly Harmony looked really sad. "I miss her a lot," she said quietly.

This shift from angry to sad surprised me. "With any luck we'll find her."

"I didn't mean my mother. My grandmother. She was a good person."

"I know she was," I said.

"How could you know that?" Harmony asked.

"She raised you, and you turned out pretty good, so she must have been a good person."

"You think I'm pretty good?"

"Don't let it go to your head, but yeah, sure, you're pretty good."

Harmony smiled, reached out and gave my hand a little squeeze. I felt embarrassed. I think she did too, because silence came between us again. I needed to break it, change the direction again.

"That was a pretty stupid assignment Ms. Gay gave us," I said.

"Which one?"

"I guess both of them."

"I saw you writing away. What did you pick to represent you, a jam sandwich?" Harmony asked.

"It sounds like some of the girls in the class think I'm pretty sweet."

"Bad joke. What did you pick?"

"A cheetah."

"Because you're so fast and elegant, have a spotted fur coat and like to eat gazelle?"

"And impalas. I put down that I kill impalas. At least tomorrow's assignment is better. It's just writing about ourselves."

"Do you really think she wants me to write about my mother being a drunk and a druggie, or you about your father being a jerk?"

Harmony didn't even know how big a jerk he was.

"Can you imagine how Ms. Gay would react if you told her the truth and wrote about what our lives are really about?" Harmony asked.

I knew she was right about that—not just about how Ms. Gay would react but also that she really didn't want us to write about the real things in our lives.

192 * ERIC WALTERS

"Of course, if you told her about your plans for university, she'd love that. Teachers like to talk about how we can all become anything we want, how the sky's the limit. That works for maybe three people in the school. The rest of us, well… we're going to be lucky to just get by."

"You'll do more than just get by," I said.

"Because I'm doing great so far, just like my mother."

We'd waded into another minefield.

"What did you choose to represent you in today's assignment?" I asked, pretending I hadn't seen the empty page she'd handed in.

"I didn't write down anything, but I did decide."

"And?" I asked.

She reached down, grabbed her backpack and started rummaging around. She pulled out a box of crayons and removed a red one. "This is me."

"You're a crayon?"

She snapped it in two. "Not a crayon. I'm a *broken* crayon."

"I don't know what that means."

"I'm broken. I'm not whole. I'm just like a broken crayon. And so are you."

"I'm not any type of crayon."

"You're certainly not a cheetah," she said.

"I'm more a cheetah than I am a crayon!"

People had turned around to look at us. I hadn't realized how loud I had gotten.

"This is one of the dumbest conversations I've ever had," I said, deliberately lowering my voice.

"It might be the *least* dumb conversation we've ever had," Harmony countered. "Are you saying your life isn't screwed up?"

Nobody had ever said anything like this to me before. I was sure some people had thought it, but none of them knew the whole truth, how bad it was. Nobody. It was part of what I had to hide. Harmony knew better. Somehow I'd told her almost all my secrets. I'd seen her as safe because she was only going to be here for a while but she'd gotten too close because she'd stayed too long.

"Okay, maybe that isn't fair," she said. "You probably aren't as screwed up as me. We had one parent each that wasn't there, even if they weren't there for different reasons. But I had a second who didn't care enough to stick around. At least, in his own strange way, your father is there."

I gasped and felt my entire body shudder.

"Are you okay?" she asked.

She'd noticed. How could she not?

I shook my head. My life was screwed up. As much as her life. Maybe more.

"My father didn't come home last night."

There. I'd said it. Words I'd never said to anybody. One of the few remaining secrets I'd kept.

"What?"

"He didn't come home last night."

"At all?"

I tried to speak, but all I could do was shake my head.

"But where was he?"

"I don't know. Sometimes he just doesn't come home."

"He's done this before."

"Yes," I whispered. "Yes."

"A lot?"

"Not a lot. A few times a year...or more some-times." If you added up the times he'd only been gone overnight, it came to eleven. Eleven times he just hadn't shown up and I was left alone.

"The first time I got taken away by child welfare, it was because my mother left me alone almost all day by myself. I don't think I have ever been so scared."

"Scared that she was dead and scared just because you were alone, right?"

"Yes, both," she said.

"I was eight the first time he left for the entire night."

Harmony let out a little stream of air, as if she were leaking. "I didn't think anybody could top my stories. And you have no idea where he is?"

"He could be anywhere. Once he called when he was more than a three-day drive away. He'd just started driving and kept going."

"At least that I understand."

"You do?" I asked.

"Sure. That's why I go on the run sometimes. I only come back if they catch me, because really, I have no place to go."

I almost said, *I have a place*. But I needed at least one secret.

"Why didn't you tell me about this last night when I called? Or at least today, before now?" she asked.

"I've never told anybody about him taking off," I said. "And you can't tell anybody else. You have to promise."

"You know I won't tell anybody. I owe you too much."

"You don't owe me anything."

"Really? Your father has taken off, and you don't know where he is or when he'll come back, and you're going with me to try to find my mother."

"At least you think you know where to find her."

She shook her head. "Your father is an even bigger jerk than I thought. The thing I don't understand is how you can be so calm."

"You get used to it, I guess. He always comes back."

"I don't mean just about this. About everything. You should be angry, like, all the time."

"I used to be."

"I heard that," she said.

"From who?"

"Mostly from Sal."

I felt a rush of anger. He'd had no right to tell her about me.

"I'd heard things about how you used to be different, so I bugged him to tell me what you were like," she said. "He didn't want to, but I kept at him until he did. He said you used to be in fights all the time."

I swallowed back my anger. No point in being angry at her or at him.

"He told me what a terror you were in school, how you got suspended for fighting in first grade, how you broke somebody's windshield with a baseball bat and how you just walked out of class sometimes."

"Sal should have shut up."

"I think he only told me so *I'd* shut up," she said. "So what changed?"

"It's hard to explain."

"We have time."

I shrugged. "Getting angry wasn't getting me anywhere. It just got me in more trouble. You'd know about that."

"Knowing it doesn't mean I can stop it. How do you do it?"

I shook my head. "I've just stopped showing how I feel."

"I don't think I could do that." She paused. "Here," she said, holding out her hand.

I held out my hand, and she dropped half of the broken crayon into it.

"What am I supposed to do with this?" I asked.

"You should just keep it. You may be even more broken than me."

I didn't want to argue anymore. Especially when I thought she was right. I tucked the piece into my pocket.

# FIFTEEN

I followed Harmony into the bar. It was the fourth place we'd been into. They were each completely different but exactly the same. Harmony explained that they all had cheap beer and a regular customer could run a "tab"—drink and pay up at the end of the month. This one, like the others, was dimly lit, had worn carpet and smelled bad.

There was some heavy metal sort of music playing. It got louder as we pushed through swinging double doors and entered into a large main room. There were lots of tables and a big bar that ran the length of the back wall. Off to the far side was a small stage. I was surprised at how many people were here already—it wasn't even six o'clock. I was glad my father hardly ever drank.

"Do you see her?" I asked.

"Not yet, but I'm pretty sure there's a back room in this place, so she might be there."

"Hey, what do you think you're doing?" a loud voice called out.

I turned to see a large, scary-looking man coming toward us.

"You kids can't be in here!"

"We're looking for my mother," Harmony said.

"I don't care if you're looking for Santa Claus! You can't be in here! We'll lose our license if an inspector comes in and sees two kids in a strip bar!"

A strip bar? Another song started playing—a Katy Perry song that I knew—and I turned around. A woman walked up onto the stage. She wasn't wearing much, and she started to dance.

"Harmony, we have to get out of here," I pleaded.

"Valerie!" Harmony screamed. "Valerie, are you here?"

People turned to look at us—at Harmony. She called out louder still. Even the woman onstage turned in our direction as she continued to dance.

"Shut up, kid. Just shut up and get out of here."

"Valerie!"

The big guy came a few steps closer, like he was going to grab her.

Harmony put up a hand and waved a finger in his face. "You touch me and I'll scream that you assaulted me. You want to explain to the police why you were touching a fourteen-year-old girl?"

He backed off, looking like he'd been scolded by his mother.

"Help me find her or convince me she isn't here, and we'll go," she said.

He nodded. "Valerie...is your mother Val Stewart?"

"Yes! Is she here?"

"She *was* here. About half an hour ago."

"Do you know where she went?"

He shook his head. "No, but the bartender might. Look, I'll go talk to him. You two wait out front, and I'll come out and tell you what he says."

"If you don't come out, we'll just come right back in," Harmony said.

"I'll come out. Just go. Please." The big scary man looked a bit scared himself.

Harmony spun around and headed for the door, leaving me staring up at the guy, who towered over me. I offered a weak little smile and headed after her. I couldn't help but look out of the corner of my eye at the stage. The dancer was already wearing less clothing than she had been a minute ago.

I caught up with Harmony just as she got to the front door. She opened it, and sunlight and fresh air flooded over us.

"At least you know your mother is okay," I said.

"She's *never* been okay. What do you know about your mother?" Harmony asked.

"Nothing, really."

"I know you were young, but your father must have told you some things about her."

"He doesn't like to talk about her."

"At all?"

I shook my head. "He says it's too hard for him to talk about her."

"He really is a jerk—a big jerk. You should be allowed to ask him questions."

"Why? What difference would it make?" I asked.

"Because then you'd know more about her. You must know something."

"I was told she was a very good person."

"At least your father told you that much."

"I didn't hear it from him. I told you he doesn't ever say anything about her, good or bad. He even put away all the pictures of her."

"You don't have a picture of her?"

"There are some in the cedar chest." When I was little I used to look at them when my father wasn't around. I hadn't done that for years.

"Do you remember anything about her?"

"I was four. So nothing."

"Not a thing?"

"Well, one thing. At least, I *think* I have one memory. It was her pushing me in a wheelbarrow."

"That's it?"

"Pretty well. She loved gardening. Our backyard used to be nothing but tulips in the spring."

"Then you remember her gardening."

"No. I was told about the gardening. Tulips come up year after year if you care for them. When I was five and six the whole backyard was blooming. But each year there were fewer and fewer, and now just a handful pop up."

"Somebody who took care of a garden would take care of her kid. You're lucky she wasn't like your father."

"How about *your* father?" I asked. "What do you know about him?"

"He was never around, right from the beginning."

"Do you know anything about him?" I asked.

"I know he was a loser."

"Your mother told you that?"

"She didn't have to. I've seen all the guys she's dated since then, and they've all been losers. Why would my father be any different?" Harmony turned and looked toward the door. "If he doesn't come out in the next two minutes, I'm going to—"

The door opened. Outside in the light of day, the man somehow looked even larger.

"Tim, he's the bartender, said he cut her off about thirty minutes ago."

"What does that mean?" Harmony asked.

"It means he wouldn't serve her any more alcohol. He told her to go get some coffee. He thought she was headed to Coffee Time. It's down that way."

"I know there's one on the corner of Broadway and Jarvis—wait, are you just making this up to get us to go away?"

"I'm not lying. Look, I got somebody to cover for me so I can walk you over."

"I think we can find it on our own," Harmony said.

"I bet you can, but I need a cup of coffee. By the way, my name is Jeff. And you are…?"

"Um, I'm Robert, and this is Harmony."

"Good to meet you."

We started walking. I still felt a bit intimidated by the guy, but it also felt like we had a bodyguard. In this neighborhood that might be a good thing.

"I didn't put it together at first," he said. "Valerie. We all call her Val."

"Yeah, that's a pretty tricky one, Val being short for Valerie. You didn't go very far in school, did you?" said Harmony.

He laughed. I hadn't expected that. "Not only do you look like her, but you sound like her too. She's pretty quick on the comebacks."

"She's even quick when she's sober, but you probably haven't seen that. So why really are you escorting us?"

"I told you. I want a coffee."

"I'm pretty sure the bar serves coffee too, so why don't you tell us the real reason?"

"Your mother didn't leave alone."

"What's his name?" Harmony asked.

"Um…Vance. How did you know it was a he?"

"It's always a he."

"Yeah. Well, Vance can get a little mean."

"Why did you let her mother leave with him?" I asked. I hadn't meant to say anything, but it just popped out.

"What was I supposed to do? Tell them they couldn't leave? Look, your girlfriend has a bit of a smart mouth, and this Vance has no sense of humor. So do you want me to come or not?"

"I'd like you along." I turned to Harmony, and she gave me a subtle nod of the head.

"Then let's go."

We walked the block without talking. As we crossed the street, I got the feeling that Jeff was leaving it up to the traffic to avoid him, not the other way around.

He held open the door to the coffee shop, and Harmony walked in. I followed. The place was almost empty.

"There she is," Harmony said. She walked—no, marched—toward a woman sitting in a corner at the back. The guy she was with looked tough. He had slicked-back hair, a scruffy beard, black leather jacket, thick black boots and torn jeans.

"I'm going to wait here," Jeff said, stopping just inside the door.

I kept walking but hung back slightly.

"Honey, what are you doing here?" Harmony's mother exclaimed. She got up from her seat and tottered a few steps, swaying as she moved. She gave Harmony an awkward hug. Harmony didn't hug her back.

"A better question is, what are *you* doing here? You're supposed to be in rehab."

Valerie giggled. What sort of a reaction was that?

"Vance, this is my daughter," she said. Her voice was rough and raspy.

"Didn't know you had any kids. You got more wear on the tires than I thought, Val."

He chuckled. Harmony's mother looked hurt.

Vance reached out to shake hands with Harmony. "Pleased to meet you."

"Can't say the same," Harmony replied, ignoring his outstretched hand. She spoke directly to her mother. "You need to get back to rehab!"

Vance grabbed Harmony's mother by the arm and pulled her roughly to her seat beside him. "Val ain't going noplace she don't want to go. Sounds like somebody should have been taught some manners," he snapped.

"You're too stupid to teach anybody anything except—"

Vance jumped to his feet and took a few steps toward Harmony. I leaped forward, putting myself between him and Harmony. He took a couple more steps, and I brought my fists up, ready to defend myself. I felt a surge of anger. He wasn't getting by me without a fight. He stopped. I was relieved and surprised all at once.

Jeff appeared out of thin air and stepped between me and Vance.

"Jeff, what are you doing here?" Vance asked, confused.

"Just came to help Harmony find her mother," he said. "How about you and I leave 'em alone to talk?"

"This isn't your bar. You can't tell me nothing about nothing in here," Vance said.

"You're right. I can't tell you to leave, but I can still squash your head like a nut. Do you want me to do that right here?"

Vance didn't answer. He stood still and scowled.

Was there going to be a fight?

Then Vance lowered his eyes and started to shuffle away. He walked past Jeff—and then right out the door.

"I'm going to make sure he goes far away," Jeff said. He turned and followed Vance outside.

Harmony sat down across from her mother. I stayed standing, giving them some space.

Even from where I stood, I could smell the alcohol coming off her.

"Don't be mad at me, honey," Valerie said. She was slurring her words, and her hair and makeup were messy.

"Why would you think I'm mad at you?" Harmony asked.

Her mother looked directly at me. "Who's this?"

"Robert is my friend, and he's here because he cared enough not to let me search for you on my own. You know, that's how responsible, caring people act."

Valerie started to cry.

I sensed somebody behind me and spun around. It was Jeff. He gave a slight nod of his head.

"You have no idea how hard it is," Valerie said through her sniffles.

"Harder than living with strangers in a friggin' foster home?" Harmony asked.

"I'm trying to get you back."

"What part of trying to get me back involves leaving rehab and going out and getting drunk?"

"I'm not drunk."

"You're so loaded they wouldn't keep serving you at the bar." Harmony looked over at Jeff. "Right?"

He nodded.

"That's just Tim being careful. I've only had a couple of drinks…three at most."

"Don't lie to me!" Harmony snapped. It sounded like Harmony was the parent and her mother was the child.

"I'm sorry," Valerie mumbled. "I love you."

"But not as much as you love getting drunk."

"Don't say that. It's just that I have a disease. Alcoholism is a disease."

"If you have a disease, you go for treatment. You don't run away from the treatment center."

Harmony wasn't giving an inch. She wasn't letting her mother's words or tears get in the way of what she wanted to say. How could anybody be that strong? I always just gave in to my father. I always thought, What's the point in arguing? It never got me anything except more grief, so I just swallowed the anger. But maybe I needed to try harder to stand my ground.

I realized Valerie's tears had stopped as suddenly as they'd started. Was it all just an act?

She grabbed a purse from the floor, opened it up and pulled out a package of cigarettes and some matches. She put a cigarette in her mouth and went to light it.

Harmony reached across the table and snatched the matches out of her mother's hand.

"You can't smoke in here. It's against the law," Harmony said.

Valerie slowly removed the cigarette from her lips and put it back into the package. "They let me smoke at rehab."

"Then maybe you should go back."

"I was thinking of going back tomorrow."

"Why not right now?" Harmony asked.

Her mother shrugged. "I have things to do and people to, you know, meet."

"Like that creep you were with?"

"He's not that bad."

"Actually, Val," Jeff said, "he's a *very* bad man. He's mean even when he's not drunk."

"That's why Jeff came along. He wanted to protect us, protect me. I'm just a stranger to him. It's not like I'm his *daughter*."

I could see her mother flinch. Another direct hit.

"You need to go back to rehab right now," Harmony said.

"We could put you in a cab or an Uber," Jeff suggested.

"I haven't got enough money for that."

"But you had enough money to keep drinking," Harmony said.

"I was drinking, but I wasn't buying." She hesitated. "Vance was buying."

"I'll pay for the ride," Jeff said.

"You'd do that?" Valerie asked. "You'd just give me the money and let me pay you back later?"

"No," he said, shaking his head. "I'm putting the Uber on my account, and it's not a loan—it's an investment. I'm investing in you getting the help you need."

"That's…that's sweet." She gave him a big smile.

"Least I can do."

She got up on unsteady feet, circled the table and hugged him. He looked uncomfortable.

"I guess I chose the wrong man in that bar," she said.

"My mother used to do that too, picking the wrong guy. Actually, I guess you're about the same age as my mother," Jeff said.

"That can't be right. She must have had you when she was a baby!" She ran her fingers through her hair like she was trying to straighten it.

"She was only nineteen. She's forty-two now."

"I'm not nearly that old!" Valerie protested. "It's just that, well, my makeup and I've been up and—"

"And you've been drinking. Alcohol makes people look older," Harmony said.

Jeff was fiddling with his phone. "There, I've ordered your ride. Let's go out front and wait."

He turned and headed for the door. Harmony took her mother by the hand and followed. I trailed behind as we walked outside.

"Thanks for doing this," Harmony said to Jeff.

"No problem." Jeff walked over to the curb to look for the Uber, and I decided to stand closer to him and leave her and her mother alone.

Jeff turned to me. "Putting yourself between Vance and Harmony takes big-time guts."

"Or small-time brains," I said.

Jeff laughed. "Guys like him are dangerous because they don't care. He wouldn't have thought twice about smacking you."

"Yeah, I figured."

"But you didn't think twice about stepping in."

"I didn't think at all or I probably wouldn't have done it. I guess I owe you a thanks too."

"You don't owe me nothing, kid. I just hope it works out," he said, gesturing to Harmony and her mother.

They were talking quietly, and Valerie was crying again. Harmony looked close to tears too.

"Look, there it is, I think," Jeff said, pointing up the street.

He raised his hand, and a red sedan pulled up to the curb in front of us. The window opened, and Jeff confirmed that the ride was for Valerie.

"You two better say goodbye. I have to get back to work. Time to go. Give the man the address," Jeff said.

Harmony and her mother exchanged a couple more words that I couldn't hear, hugged and then Valerie got into the car. It drove off, and Jeff and I both stepped up beside Harmony and watched it disappear around the corner.

"Do you think she'll make it?" I asked Jeff.

"We put her in the vehicle and she's headed in the right direction."

"That doesn't mean anything," Harmony said. "She might just have him drive her to another bar."

"She might. It's up to her. Not me. Not you. Not the people at the rehab center. It's all up to her. Remember that. Now, you two, where do you live?"

"The West End," I said. "St. Clair and Old Weston Road."

"I'm going to call another Uber for the two of you."

"We don't have the money to pay for it," I said.

"This one's on me too."

"We can take the subway," I suggested.

"Not if you want to get home before dark."

"Why are you doing this?" Harmony asked.

"Maybe I'm just a nice guy."

"Is it because your mother was an alcoholic?" I asked.

He smiled. "You're not just gutsy but also smart."

"He's the smartest person in our school," Harmony said. "Well…is he right?"

Jeff nodded. "At least half right. My mother is *still* an alcoholic. One who hasn't had a drink in over seven years. Once an alcoholic, always an alcoholic."

He turned directly to Harmony. "Some people make it. You have to have faith. Especially when it seems like there's nothing else. And remember, it's not on you. It's up to her."

# SIXTEEN

We hardly said a word the whole ride home. The Uber driver filled in the silence by talking and talking and talking. I felt like we were trapped in his car. We had him stop and pull over a block from Harmony's house. We couldn't risk Mrs. Watson seeing us get out of an Uber or she'd know something was wrong and that we'd lied.

Our timing worked out almost perfectly. We got to her place at about the time we would have if we'd really had supper at my place and studied for a while.

"I want to thank you," said Harmony.

"I couldn't let you go alone."

"You know that guy could have killed you. What were you thinking?"

"I wasn't thinking. I was just…just…well… I was just…"

"Angry?" Harmony asked.

I shook my head. "More than angry."

"Hard to keep that stuff inside all the time. Do you think your father is going to be there when you get home?"

"I don't know. It doesn't matter."

"It *does* matter. And if he isn't there?" she asked.

"I walk the dog, eat supper and wait."

"If he isn't there, I want you to call me," she said.

"Sure, but either way, I'm okay." One more night would pass. One more day was already over.

"Either way, you should call. See you tomorrow."

"You too."

"And again, thanks for coming."

"Friends help friends. You can't choose your family, but you can choose your friends."

She laughed. "My grandmother used to say that. You know, you remind me of her."

"Great. Just what I always wanted to hear, that I remind a girl of her grandmother."

"I meant it as a compliment."

"How else could I take it? See you tomorrow."

I started to walk away.

"Robert!"

I stopped and turned, and she walked over to me.

"Do you know why you can't be my boyfriend?"

"Because it would be strange to date somebody who reminds you of your grandmother?"

"That's one reason, but not the main reason. It's just that I can't risk it."

"So now it's *me* who's dangerous?"

She laughed. "Hardly anybody knows how funny you are."

"Yet another reason not to date me."

"You're not that funny. It's just…have you ever seen a boy-and-girl thing that didn't go bad?"

"Some work."

"Almost all of them don't. You're too important to me to risk it."

She spun around and walked off, leaving me standing there watching as she went inside and the door closed behind her.

Now I had to go home. I'd spent most of the day and all evening not thinking about my father. School had helped with that. Going off with Harmony had kept my mind elsewhere for almost the whole evening. Now there was nothing else to keep it occupied. I'd soon turn the corner and either his car would be there or it wouldn't. I'd know in just a few more paces. I held my breath and my hopes and—there it was. His car was there.

I stopped, exhaled and then took a deep breath. It was like a weight had been lifted off my shoulders. He was back. I wasn't going to be alone tonight.

I quietly crossed the porch and opened the door. Candy came running, barking to greet me. I bent down and took her head in my hands, scratching her behind her ears. I could hear the TV.

"I'm home!" I called out.

There was no answer. If he'd been up all last night and today, he might be asleep in front of the set. If that was the case, it might be better—and easier—to just let him sleep. I put down my pack and looked into the living room. He was awake and watching TV.

"Hey," I said softly.

He looked over. "Hang on," he said.

I stood there and waited as he kept watching his TV show. It was a sitcom, and he was chuckling at some of the jokes. That was a good sign, although the show really wasn't funny or important enough that I should have to stand there and wait. I felt something rising in the pit of my stomach. He'd been gone all night, and now he was back and wanted me to wait for him. Who did he think he was? I had to fight the urge to yell at him or go over and turn off the TV or—a commercial came on.

"Where were you?" he asked.

"I was out with a friend."

"Okay."

I waited for him to say more, but he just stared at the TV.

"That must be one great commercial," I said.

He looked up at me.

"Don't you have anything else to say? Aren't you even curious where I was?" I asked.

He didn't answer. His expression didn't even change.

"I've been out with Harmony since school ended. We went to the east end of the city."

"That explains why *I* had to peel potatoes."

That's what I got. He didn't care that I'd been on the other side of the city or why. Instead it was about how this had caused him to have to do something.

"I had Sal let Candy out."

"I don't like strangers in the house."

"He's not a stranger. He's my friend."

"I don't like anybody in the house. Were you working?"

"I just told you I was out with Harmony in the *East* End."

"Oh yeah." The show was back on, and he stared at the TV again.

"If I had been working, I wouldn't be home until nine thirty. That's when I come home when I'm working."

"I don't keep track of everything you do."

"You don't keep track of *anything* I do!" I snapped.

"What's your problem?"

At least I'd gotten him to turn away from the TV. He was glaring at me.

I shouldn't have said that. I wanted to retreat, not provoke him. I wanted to look away or even apologize. Harmony wouldn't have done any of those things. She was too brave to back off.

"My problem is you," I said quietly.

"What did you say?" he demanded.

I'd had enough. "You're my problem. Where were you last night?" I demanded.

"Where I was is my business. I'm the parent and you're the kid."

"Parents don't just disappear overnight and leave a child alone."

"Excuse me for thinking you are more responsible than some *child*. I thought I'd raised you better than that."

"You've hardly raised me at all. It's like I was brought up by wolves—no, that's not right, because wolves probably take care of their young."

He jumped up from his chair. He brushed by me and walked toward the front door.

I went after him. "What are you doing?"

"I'm going out."

I grabbed him by the arm. "Where are you going? When are you coming back?"

"I guess you'll see, won't you?"

I let go of his arm and walked to the door. I opened it up.

"If you're not back by eleven, I'm going to call Uncle Jack and Aunt Cora."

"And tell them what?"

"Everything. I'm going to tell them everything. About the times you leave me alone."

"And what do you think that will do?" he asked.

"I'm going to ask them to come and get me. I'm going to ask them if I can go and live with them."

He laughed. "Like that's going to happen. Why would anybody want to care for you? You're lucky I'm still around."

"Yeah, I'm really lucky!" I yelled.

He looked at me long and hard, and then he smiled and chuckled. "Believe what you want. Believe your aunt and uncle will come and rescue you. Give it a try, and see who's right."

"Maybe I'm wrong. Maybe they won't come, but they'll call the police instead. Maybe I'll call the police. I'll tell them that I'm alone and that you've done it before."

"Sure you will."

"I will. I'll do it."

"Go ahead. You'll end up in some foster home, and I'll end up being rid of you. You don't think my life would be better without you?"

I felt that jab directly in my head. But I didn't change my expression.

"Maybe your life would be better. I just know it has to change. *You* have to change. If you're not home by eleven, I'm calling."

He didn't look so confident anymore, but he didn't look convinced either. Did he think I was bluffing? I didn't know myself. What had I started? Whatever it was, I wasn't going to let it end partway through.

"If you *ever* leave me alone all night again, I'm making that phone call. Not just tonight. Any night. If you ever do it again, I'll call."

"You do what you have to do, and I'll do what I have to do."

He walked by me and through the door. He took a few steps toward the car, then turned and started walking up the street. He was going, but he probably wasn't going too far or for too long. I hadn't won the game, but I hadn't lost. He'd be back tonight. Probably.

I closed the door. I didn't have time to worry. I had homework to do. But first I had to call Harmony and let her know that my father was home. Then I decided I should wait until he came back again before I called. That is, *if* he came home again. And if he didn't, would I make the call to my aunt and uncle or the police? I knew that whoever I called, nothing would ever be the same again.

1,614 1,613

# SEVENTEEN

Harmony was sitting on the curb when I came up to her house.

"You're late!" she snapped.

I looked at my watch. I was actually a few minutes early.

She got up and started walking. I fell in beside her, and we walked together in silence.

"You didn't call last night, so was he there?" she asked.

"He was home, but he didn't get there until it was too late to call you."

I'd actually forgotten. My dad was gone for almost two hours after our blowout. He got back just before eleven—before the deadline. He went straight to bed without talking to me. I figured he thought that was some sort of punishment for me. It was more of a relief. What I still didn't know was whether I was bluffing about the phone call. If he'd been fifteen minutes late, would I have called, or would I have waited until he'd been gone all night? I wasn't sure, but I had decided I was going to call my aunt and uncle after school today just to say hello. It had been a while and it would be nice to talk to them.

"Did he tell you where he was?" she asked.

"I didn't ask, and he didn't tell."

"So he just strolls in as if nothing happened and he wasn't gone."

"That's pretty well it."

"And he doesn't say, 'I'm sorry' or 'Are you okay?' or anything?"

"Nothing."

"Even my mother apologizes. Actually, she apologizes all the time. Sometimes she wakes me up in the middle of the night to apologize to me for all the things she's done wrong."

"And does it mean anything?" I asked.

Harmony shook her head.

"I'm just glad we found her," I said. "Do you think she did go to the rehab center?"

"I won't know until the social worker calls and tells my foster mother—assuming I'm even talking to my foster mother today."

Okay, that explained why Harmony was waiting on the curb. "You got into a fight with Mrs. Watson?"

"No, she got into a fight with me."

"What happened?" I asked.

"She wouldn't let me have any space. She kept bugging me at breakfast, asking questions."

"What sort of questions?"

"How was I doing at school, what things did I need her to buy, new clothes or school supplies or—"

"What a terrible human being. No wonder you had to leave."

"Shut...right...up. She was getting way too personal. She was asking about friends, about my mother."

"Maybe she's asking because she cares," I suggested.

"She cares about the money. She wanted to

know if I'd be happy to stay there for the rest of the school year or longer. I think they're counting on the money."

"Or maybe they like having you around. No, wait, that couldn't *possibly* be the reason. Who in their right mind would want to have you around? No wonder you were waiting on the curb. Should we call the police to report them as dangerous?"

"You're going to miss me when I'm gone."

I suddenly realized just how much I *was* going to miss her. How had this person, this *girl*, become so important in my life so fast? I couldn't allow myself to think this way.

"You know, there are phones. We could still call each other," Harmony said.

I didn't answer. It wouldn't be the same.

"Do you think you're going to be here for a while?" I asked.

"It depends on my mother."

"Yesterday was a good start. You got her back into rehab."

"All we did was get her into an Uber. She could have jumped out before she got there."

"Do you think that's possible?"

"Alcoholics can't be trusted."

Some people who aren't alcoholics also can't be trusted, I thought, but I didn't say it.

"We'll hope she's in rehab," I said.

Or hope she *did* jump out of the Uber, so that Harmony would be able stay here longer. I instantly felt terrible for just thinking that. Harmony wanted to go home even if it was a terrible home. I understood that better than anybody. Shouldn't I want that for her?

"Darlene really likes you," Harmony said.

"I like her too."

"No, I mean she *really* likes you."

"Could you break it to her that she's a bit old for me and I wouldn't want to date a married woman?"

"You think you are *so* funny."

"You're the one who keeps telling me that," I said.

"What I'm trying to say is that if you had to come into foster care, the Watsons' would be a good place for you to live."

"I'm not going into foster care."

"You don't know that. It could happen."

Should I tell her that I'd threatened my father with that the night before?

"If your father keeps taking off, it might be what happens to you whether you want it or not."

"Nobody knows about him taking off. Only you, and you're not going to tell anybody, right?"

"You know that."

Did I? Could I really trust her?

"It's just that if he was gone for a long time, you couldn't survive on your own."

"Yes, I could. I could be on my own for a long time. You've seen how much food there is in the basement. There's money to pay the bills. It could last for months."

And each day got me closer.

"There are worse things than living with the Watsons," she said.

"*You're* the one who should keep that in mind."

"All I'm saying is, sometimes things happen that you can't control. It could happen to you," she said.

"I'm fine. I've got a plan."

"To stay at home and eat the groceries from the basement until there's none left?" she snapped.

"That's part of the plan."

"It's a stupid plan. Do you think anybody is going to let a thirteen-year-old live on his own?"

"They will if they don't know."

"Somebody will find out," she said.

"No, they won't. The neighbors don't notice. The only person who knows anything is you. Besides, that's only part of the plan."

"And what's the rest of the plan?" she demanded.

I opened my mouth to speak and then stopped myself. I couldn't reveal the rest of it. That was my top-secret backup plan nobody could know about. Or could I tell her? Could I trust her? Before I could decide, she jumped back in.

"Are you just talking, or do you actually have another plan?"

I thought again about telling her. If I could tell anybody, it would be her.

"Either you have more of a plan and you're not going to tell me, or you don't have a plan and you're a liar. Either way you're a jerk, and I don't have time for jerks!"

She spun on her heels and walked onto the road, causing a car to blow its horn at her and slow down. She crossed over to the other side and kept walking. I stood there, stunned. Should I go after her, call out or…let her walk away? One of us was being a jerk, and I was pretty sure it wasn't me.

✱

At lunchtime I sat down at my usual spot at the table, right beside Harmony. She didn't say hello or turn in my direction. I wasn't surprised. She hadn't talked to me during or after basketball practice, or looked my way during the entire morning of classes.

Everybody else greeted me. Did they notice she hadn't? We all pulled out our lunches. Harmony and I hadn't exchanged food on the way to school, and I got the feeling it wasn't going to happen now either. I saw she had a roast beef sandwich on brown bread, and it had little bits of green sticking out the sides. I, of course, had jam. I was the king of jam sandwiches.

It was strange sitting there while Harmony made conversation with all the guys and completely ignored me.

"Are you guys going to the party tonight?" Taylor asked.

"Of course," Raj replied.

"Wouldn't miss it," Sal said.

"What party?" I asked.

"It's at Devon's place," Jay explained.

"Although it's more his brother's party," Taylor added.

Devon's older brother was in high school. I'd seen him around the neighborhood but didn't really know him.

"Do you know what that means?" Raj asked.

"High school girls," Sal said, and the two of them gave each other a high five.

"And we all know what *that* means," Taylor said.

"That you all have the opportunity to be rejected by older girls," Harmony said.

I couldn't help but laugh.

"Things could happen," Taylor said.

"Yeah, you keep believing that," Harmony said. "It's a fine line between confidence and delusion and you two have crossed over."

"Anyway," Taylor said, ignoring Harmony, "his brother told Devon he could invite people as long as he doesn't tell their parents there was a party at their house while they were away."

"Their parents aren't going to be there?" I asked.

"That's why they're having a party," Jay said.

"And that's going to make it a *real* party," Taylor said.

"So are all of you going?" I asked.

They nodded.

"Devon didn't even mention it to me," I said.

"He probably thought you wouldn't come."

"Why would he think that?"

"Because you're always working or studying. Besides, it could get a little wild," Taylor explained.

"I could get wild," I said.

They all chuckled and exchanged looks that left no doubt they didn't believe what I'd just said.

"Then you should come," Jay said.

"I can't. I'm working until nine," I explained.

"Like I said, you're working," Taylor said.

"You could come after work. It's not even going to get started much before then," Jay said.

I was going to mention that after work I had a couple of hours of studying to do, but I thought that would just prove them even more right.

"You should come," Raj added. "We'll all be there."

"I don't know," I said. "Sometimes I have to stay later at the store to clean up. By the time I got home and got changed and got there, the party would be almost over."

"I don't think it's going to be over until the middle of the night. It would be good to have you there. Just think about it," Taylor said.

"Sure." But I wasn't going to think about it, and I wasn't going to go.

"I don't know Devon very well, but can I go too?" Harmony asked.

"For sure," Sal said.

"Awesome."

"Cool. Then we'll see you there," Jay said. "Or maybe it would be better for me to swing around and get you. Would that be okay?"

"That would be nice," Harmony said.

"Okay, how about around eight thirtyish?"

"Perfect. I'll see you then." Harmony stood up, grabbed her stuff and left. We watched her walk away.

"Have you two broken up?" Jay asked.

"Of course not. I mean, we weren't together to break up."

"But you are having a fight," Sal said.

"*I'm* not having a fight."

"Then it won't bother you that she'll be at the party," Taylor said.

"She can go where she wants," I said.

"Or that she's going with *me* to the party," Jay said.

I almost told him he was crazy, but everybody laughed, so I didn't have to say anything.

"You're *walking* with her, but you're not *going* with her," Taylor said.

"That's for sure," Sal added.

The bell rang. That was the end of things. At least, for now.

⋅ ⋆ ⋅

Harmony was walking slightly ahead of me on the other side of the road. She had spent the afternoon on the edge of disaster, looking for a fight with everybody and anybody. Well, except me, because she didn't even look in my direction.

I'd thought some more about going to the party, but mostly I'd thought about Harmony—or, rather, something she'd said to me the other day about my friends not really being my friends. She was so wrong. They weren't the ones who didn't talk to me at lunch. They were my friends long before she showed up, and they'd be my friends long after she was gone.

Then my father's words came tumbling back: "Friends come and go. You can't count on them. You can't count on anybody but yourself. Don't ever forget that. Counting on people is counting on being disappointed."

Did you need friends? Were they only there to disappoint you? Maybe my father was right, and all you could count on was yourself. So what if Harmony wasn't talking to me? Big deal if she never talked to me again. Big deal if she left. The sooner she left, the sooner my secrets were safe. Talking to her, letting her get close, had been a big mistake.

Rockwell Avenue was just up ahead. She'd turn right to get to Silverthorn, and I'd turn left to get to Chambers. That's where we'd part. She was still slightly ahead. That meant she'd turn and leave me before I turned and left her. People leaving wasn't as big a threat for me as it was for other people. Life went on. Life would go on after she was gone.

She made the turn. I made my turn. I didn't look back to see if she was looking back. It didn't matter. I had work to do and a plan to follow, and she wasn't part of that plan. Maybe on Monday morning I could even leave a few minutes later for school, since I wouldn't have to make a detour to walk with her.

# EIGHTEEN

I looked at my watch as I left the house. It was almost ten. It had taken me longer to get cleaned up and dressed than I'd thought it would. I had put on my only good pair of pants—the ones I'd bought with Harmony. In the five-block walk I'd changed my mind five times about going. But I was still moving in that direction. At least part of the reason I was going was because Harmony was going to be there. I'd decided I wanted to talk to her. Her being stupid with me didn't mean I should be stupid with her. Besides, I needed to know.

Now, still half a block away, I could hear the party. I got closer and it got louder. Right out front there were five people standing on the lawn

—three guys and two girls—all of them holding red plastic cups. They were older, probably Devon's brother's friends.

"Are you a friend of Gavin's?" one of the guys asked me.

"No."

"Then buzz off. This is private."

"I'm a friend of his brother, Devon. He invited me."

"Okay, then go around the side—the party is in the backyard."

As I rounded the back of the house, I could feel the bass pounding through the ground. And then I stopped, stunned. The backyard was filled with people. There had to be more than a hundred people crammed in here. A stone patio off to one side was being used as a dance floor, and it looked even more packed than the rest of the yard. Overhead, Christmas lights were strung on poles. It was sort of pretty.

I was relieved when I saw the guys, and I waved at them. Jay, Taylor, Sal and Raj rushed toward me, waving their arms in the air.

"Robbie, my man!" Taylor yelled and then surprised me by giving me a big hug. I smelled alcohol.

"We didn't think you were going to show, Robert," Jay said.

"I told you I had to finish work," I yelled back over the music.

"Just glad you got here before I have to leave," Sal added.

"You're leaving?"

"Not yet, but I have to be home by eleven, so I only have a while."

"And you guys?" I asked the others.

"I'm good until midnight," Taylor said.

"Me too. Midnight," Jay replied.

"I have a one-in-the-morning curfew," Raj said. "And you?"

"Midnight." That was a lie. I could be out all night if I wanted.

"You should get something to drink," Taylor said, holding up his red plastic cup.

"Yeah, you should!" Jay agreed. "It's a very special punch!"

I could smell the "special."

"You have some catching up to do," Sal said and then took a big slurp from his cup to prove his point.

"Sure. So...is Harmony here?" I asked.

"She came with me," Jay said.

"I don't see her," I said.

"I haven't seen her for a while either," Taylor said.

"The party's so big it spilled out of the backyard and into the alley," Raj explained.

"Do you think that's where she is?"

"Probably, but I thought you and Harmony weren't talking," Taylor said.

"She's not talking to me. That doesn't mean I'm not talking to her. Lead the way."

"Don't you want a drink first?" Taylor asked.

"I'll get one later."

"No need for later. I can go and get you one," Sal said.

"Sure, thanks."

I didn't want anything to drink, but what could I say? Drinking made no sense to me. I was working hard to be in control of my life—I couldn't risk losing that control.

Sal headed off in one direction while the rest of us went the other, weaving our way through the crowd. The people were older than us—some a lot older—and they were loud. It was obvious they had had a lot of punch to drink. I was uneasy. The whole place gave me the feeling that people were on the edge of losing it.

We gave a wide berth to a couple of guys who were yelling at each other. Judging from the way a crowd was starting to form around them, I knew I wasn't the only one who thought this could lead to something more. We'd only gone a few steps past them when there was a roar and somebody yelled, "Fight, fight!" A rush of people moved in their direction.

I pushed through, then turned and saw that my friends weren't following. They had joined the crowd watching the fight. The back gate was open, and people were running into the yard from the alley, hoping to catch the action. I waited until there was an opening and then popped through and out into the alley. It was instantly much darker, the only light coming from a lamppost halfway down the block on the main road.

The people in the alley were spread out, and I couldn't see if Harmony was one of them. Maybe she'd already left and gone home. That would have been the smart thing to do, which meant she was probably still here. Being here in this alley in the dark wasn't that smart either, but I couldn't leave without trying to talk to her. Harmony was in my head. I'd been thinking about her all during my work shift. If this was the end of us being friends, I at least wanted to know. I was tired of waiting for things to happen and having no control.

There seemed to be more people to my left, so I headed that way. There were little clusters of people standing beside and between the garages along the alley. I looked at the first group—and they looked at me. They were definitely older and bigger than me. One of them scowled at me. I quickly looked away. I flashed back to the last time I was in an alley and then started wondering if those guys could be here tonight. That thought got me spooked. I wanted to just turn around and leave. And then I saw her—at least, I thought I did. Her back was turned to me.

"Harmony?" I called out.

She turned around. She was standing in the shadows with four other people, one of them a girl and all of them older than Harmony. She was holding a red plastic cup. They were all holding those red cups. Was I the only person not drinking?

"Um, can we talk?" I asked.

"I doubt I could stop you if I tried," she replied.

"I was hoping we could talk alone."

"Who is this kid?" one of the guys asked.

"He's a friend," Harmony said.

"Friend or boyfriend?" one of the other guys asked.

"Boyfriend?" she scoffed. "*Look* at him. Give me a break. Do you think I'd have *him* as a boyfriend?"

They all laughed—laughed at me. I hadn't expected her to say that or that it would hurt so much.

"Then you should tell your friend that people came here to party!" He yowled, and two of them exchanged a high five.

"Please, Harmony. It's important."

"I don't want to talk."

"Just for a minute, please."

"The girl said she didn't want to talk," the biggest guy said. "You need to leave."

"Harmony?"

Her expression softened. "Sure, we can talk."

The big guy grabbed her by the arm as she started to walk away. "Stay with us."

"Let her go!" I yelled.

Judging by his expression, I had surprised him as much as I'd surprised myself.

"Or what are you going to do about it?" he demanded. "Are you going to fight me?"

"Yes."

He laughed. They all laughed except Harmony. He released her arm.

"Do you really think you can take me, you little puke?" he asked.

I shook my head. "That doesn't matter. I'll still fight you if I have to."

"It looks like you have to," he said. He reached out and gave me a poke in the chest. "Just walk away while you can."

I felt the hairs on the back of my neck go up, and a lump formed in my chest. A lump of anger.

"Maybe *you* should walk away while *you* still can," I said.

His friends all laughed, but this time it was at him. He looked as angry as I felt.

"I'm not afraid of you," I said.

"You should be." He pushed both hands hard against my chest, and I stumbled backward and fell onto one knee.

I got up. I brushed my hand against the knee of my pants, worried that it had ripped. It was fine. I knew I should walk away but I couldn't. Instead I stepped toward him. He pushed me again, and this time I almost tumbled right over and onto the ground.

I walked back toward him again. This time I put up my fists.

"Don't make me do this to you," he said. His voice had changed. He wasn't threatening as much as he was pleading. "Just walk away while you can."

I shook my head. "I'm not walking away without Harmony."

"Come on, Josh, he's just a kid—leave him alone," the girl said.

"Talk to him," he said to the girl. "He's the one looking for a fight."

"What grade are you in?" the girl asked me.

"Eighth. Just like Harmony."

They looked surprised, and all of them turned to Harmony.

"You're in eighth grade?" the big guy—Josh —asked.

"Yeah, so what?" Harmony asked.

"I'm in eleventh—we're all in eleventh grade. I thought you were in high school."

"We better go," the girl said. "Leave them to talk and—shoot! The police!"

I spun around. There were flashing lights, and two—no, three—police cars were bumping up the alley toward us.

I reached out and grabbed Harmony's hand. "Come on," I yelled and dragged her away. The others followed, like I knew where I was going. A few more joined in, running with us down the alley and away from the flashing lights—and then another set of flashing lights was coming at us from the other direction! We skidded to a stop. People froze in place, captured by the beams of the oncoming squad car. We were trapped!

Without saying a word, I led Harmony away from the group and into a gap between two garages. There was a chain-link gate. I opened it and we went into the backyard. I closed the gate behind me. It was empty and quiet and dark.

"Where are we going?" Harmony asked.

"Away from the police. This is a good place to hide."

It was then that I noticed she was still holding a plastic cup. I took the cup from her hand. "I think you've had enough already." She didn't protest as I dropped it to the ground and it splashed back up onto me.

The house we were hiding behind was dark—no lights, no motion. Everybody was either out or asleep. This wasn't the worst place to hide, but what if the police started checking the yards around Devon's house? We had to get farther away. I led her down the narrow space between the two houses. Still in the shadows, I peeked out at the street. There were a couple of police cars, some officers on foot and kids on the street, but they were all down the way by Devon's place.

"Can you run?" I asked.

"What sort of stupid question is that?"

"You're not even walking that well. How much have you had to drink?"

"That's not your business."

"It is if we get caught. Okay, let's go."

We came out from between the houses and hit the street running. We weren't alone. There were other kids running down the street along with us. I kept dragging Harmony along until we hit the end of the block and turned the corner.

"I need to stop," Harmony said.

I slowed us down to a jog. "We need to keep moving."

She dug in her heels, and we came to a stop. "I need to do something else."

She bent over and hurled. The smell of alcohol swept over us.

"Are you all right?" I asked.

She answered by vomiting again. There was nothing but liquid, and the smell of alcohol and vomit was overpowering. She wiped her mouth against her sleeve.

"I need to sit down," she said.

"There's a parkette just up ahead. There's a bench. Come on."

I grabbed her hand again and we walked up the street and into the parkette. It was a little square of green with a bench and a small flower bed. It was dark and empty, and I was relieved. We could sit here unseen. I led her over to the bench, and we sat down. I let go of her hand and we sat there in silence, in the dark, for a while.

"I'm a jerk," she said.

I didn't answer.

"This is where you're supposed to disagree and tell me that I'm *troubled*. That's what the social workers always say about me, that I'm troubled."

"Just because you're troubled doesn't mean you can't be a jerk too," I said. "A drunken jerk."

"Okay, I deserved that. I need to tell you something. The social worker called and told me that my mother went back to rehab."

"That's great news!"

"And left again the next morning."

"I'm sorry. Do you want me to come with you to go looking for her again?"

"You'd do that?"

"If you want me to."

"Thanks, but really, what's the point?" she asked.

I guessed there wasn't any point, and I was grateful she didn't want to.

"Tomorrow's Saturday, so you're working, right?"

"All day until closing, but I'm home by six. Do you want to hang out? I have homework to do—we both have homework to do. We could watch some TV after."

"What about your father?"

"It's Saturday night, so he'll be out," I said.

"Then that would be nice. I really am sorry."

"That's okay. We all do stupid things."

"Do you do stupid things?" she asked.

"I just offered to fight a guy who was twice as big as me."

"That was stupid. That's twice in a few days you've done that," she said.

"You really are a bad influence." I took a breath. "Look, I'm sorry about your mother."

"And I'm sorry for calling you a liar about having a plan. You're about the only person who doesn't lie to me."

"Don't worry about that now. Right now we need to get you home. When is your curfew?"

"Eleven thirty."

"Then we can definitely get you home in time. You need to get straight upstairs and to bed so they won't know you were drinking."

"Yeah, maybe that will work. I just feel so stupid."

"Good. Maybe you won't do this again."

"It doesn't seem to have stopped me from getting drunk before," she said. "Do you know what the worst thing is?"

"That you vomited on your shoes?"

She chuckled ever so slightly. "The worst thing is, I'm doing the things my mother did when she was my age…that she still does…and I'm starting to think I'm just like her."

"You're nothing like her," I protested.

"Drunk and hanging out with some loser in an alley?" she asked.

"This is a park, and I'm not a loser."

"I meant back there…oh, you're joking."

"Apparently not well, but yes."

"What I'm saying is, is she who I'm going to become?"

"No."

"You don't know her, and you really don't know me."

"I *do* know you, and I know you can become anything you want to become."

"I'm not like you."

"And you're not like her either. You're you. You're smart and—"

"Not like you," she said.

"The only difference between you and me is that I work hard. And you can too. You just need to plan. Do you still want to know what my backup plan is?"

"You don't have to tell me if you don't want to."

"I know I don't have to, but I'm going to. And I'm not going to tell you—I'm going to show you. Tomorrow. Right now let's get you home."

# NINETEEN

Mrs. Priamo had let me leave work a bit early. I'd rushed away, run home as fast as I could, washed up and changed. I was now wearing my new pants, socks without holes, and a shirt. They were clean. *All* my clothes were clean. While I was at work my father had done the laundry. He'd also cleaned the house and gone grocery shopping. He was halfway down in the elevator, and things were calm. Times like these gave me hope that somehow the elevator would get stuck right there in the middle.

Supper had been waiting for me when I got home—mashed potatoes, a can of creamed corn and a quarter tin of ham. We didn't usually have anything that fancy. I liked ham. It wasn't like my father went to much trouble, but the fact that he'd made it and had it waiting for me meant a lot. Then he had gotten all dressed up and driven off for his night out.

Every Saturday night for as long as I could remember, my father had gone to a dance at a local hall. There was a band and people he knew, and that was what they did every Saturday. They went out and talked and danced and drank a little. He drank vodka.

When I was little and he was going out, I always tried to get myself "ready" before he left. I'd take whatever food and drink I wanted to have and lock myself and Candy into his bedroom, where I could watch TV and try not to worry about being alone. Of course, I was older now and didn't need to do that.

Candy started barking before the knock came on the door. She was louder than a knock and better than an alarm system. I assumed Harmony had arrived. I peeked through the window. It was her.

"It's okay, girl," I said to Candy. "It's Harmony."

I opened the door and pulled Candy away to let Harmony in. She greeted Candy first. She held out her hand, and there was a little dog treat. She always brought Candy a treat—a small piece of meat she'd saved from her dinner. Candy grabbed it and ran off to eat it in solitude.

"I didn't see the car, so your father's gone, right?" Harmony asked.

"About twenty minutes ago, and we're going too," I said. "Come on."

We squeezed out the door and Harmony started down the walk.

"This way," I said.

I went around the side of the house, opened the door to the shed and walked in. Harmony watched and waited, looking confused. I took a big pack off a hook. It was heavy, and the weight made me feel good. I heaved it onto my back.

"Now we can go," I said.

I walked out of the shed, closed the door and started walking. Harmony was soon at my side.

"What's in the pack?" she asked.

"You'll find out when we get there. Did the Watsons figure out you'd been drinking?"

"I think Darlene knew, but she pretended not to notice. She also apologized to me."

"For what?"

"She said she knew it must be hard to go through what I'm going through and she'd try to give me a little more space. You know, it's not the worst place to be."

We came up to the railroad tracks and walked beside them for a while. We got to the right spot, and I climbed up the embankment with Harmony beside me. We stopped right by the fence. I looked both ways to see if anybody was watching. We were alone. I removed two loosely placed metal clips and pulled back the wire mesh on a section of fence to create an opening big enough for us to get through.

I motioned at Harmony. "Go ahead."

Harmony went first. Then me, my pack just clearing the opening. I turned around, pulled the mesh back into place and put the clips back on, sealing it up again. I looked around. Still nobody watching.

"It's not that far now," I said.

We crossed over the main tracks and then the other two sets of tracks. Those were side rails where an engine would bring a car or two of raw materials to a factory or take away finished goods. We moved down the embankment on the other side. At the bottom there was a small creek. It ran out of a big sewer grate a few blocks north. The water was low, so we could step on the big stones in the middle to cross.

Harmony looked uneasy. That was something I didn't see very often. We continued moving until we hit a patch of forest. It wasn't big—not anything that could even be called a forest, really, but just an area of trees and bushes here in the city, by the tracks and abandoned factories. We followed a little path to a small clearing.

"Here we are," I said.

"Okay, but I still don't know why we're here."

"What can you see?" I asked.

She looked around. "Trees, brush and some condos farther away. The top floors of a couple of deserted factories. Basically...nothing."

"Nothing is important."

I put down my pack, and it clattered. I opened it up and pulled out the first thing I was looking for—a collapsible chair. I unfolded it and clicked it into place, then offered it to Harmony.

"Have a seat," I said. She sat down.

I started pulling more items out of the bag. There was a flashlight that had a crank so it didn't need batteries, a stove that operated on propane, a couple of extra fuel canisters, and some pots and pans.

"Are we having a cookout?" Harmony asked.

I pulled out a sleeping bag. "Or a sleepover. This is a special thermal fleece-lined bag guaranteed to keep somebody warm camping in subzero temperatures."

"Let me guess. There's a tent in there too."

I pulled out the tent. "Winter-certified two-person Arctic survival tent in camouflage green. It blends into the trees and is easy to set up."

I took it and basically flung it into the air, and it popped open as a full-fledged tent. It was like a magic trick.

"That's a pretty amazing tent."

"And completely waterproof. There can be a storm outside, and you're safe and dry inside. I know that for a fact because I've been in it during a big thunderstorm. I also have a shovel, an ax and a cooler in my shed that I can bring along. This is my final backup plan."

"What are you talking about?"

"We're in the middle of our neighborhood, surrounded by tens of thousands of people, and we're completely isolated. I could live here and nobody would know it."

"What do you mean, live here?"

"I could stay here. I could live right here."

"You can't be serious."

"I am. It works. I've slept out here."

"By yourself?"

"Of course by myself. I needed to make sure the equipment all worked. I needed to make sure it was as isolated here as I thought it was. I've done it a few times. Once for three days."

"And your father just let you go camping on your own?"

"I told him I was staying at a friend's house. He doesn't know about this place because nobody does. Nobody but you. Nobody knows about this plan. Nobody but you."

She looked confused but like she was trying to think.

"So, if I understand, your plan is to go and live by yourself in a tent by the railroad tracks?" she finally said.

"This is my backup plan. Well, really, my *backup* backup plan. My plan is to survive living with my father as long as I can or at least live in the house without him as long as nobody knows. Then, when somebody finds out, I'll come here to live."

"Look, staying here for a few days is one thing, but you don't actually believe you can live here forever, do you?" Harmony asked.

"Not forever."

I reached into the pack and pulled out one more thing—my notebook. I'd put in there before Harmony arrived. I handed it to her.

"Open it up. Turn to the last page I've written on and tell me what it says."

She did. "It's a number—1,612. What does it mean?"

"That's the number of days between now and the time I can go to university."

"How do you know that?"

"I counted them. I'm counting down to my end date, the day I have to get to. It's how long I have to survive everything."

"You can't live out here. It would be impossible," she said.

"I hope I don't have to. I'll keep living with my father as long as I can—until he leaves or dies or whatever. Then I'll live in the house without him."

"There's no way anybody will let you live on your own."

"If he just disappears, nobody will know. I'll pay the bills and run the house. I'll go to school and work at the butcher shop. I have the banking information. I can just keep living there. Maybe for six months or even a year, if I do it right, and each day will be a day closer to the end. If he disappeared today, it would only be 1,612 days more."

"You couldn't last that long."

"Why not? I've already lasted over 3,000 days."

"What?"

"When my mother died, I had 5,012 days to go."

I took the book from her and opened it to the first page. The very first number written there was 5,012.

"Come on, you didn't start counting days back when you were four," Harmony said.

"Of course not. I've only been counting days for two years. I went back and figured it out and crossed out each day that I'd already lived. I've lasted almost twice as many days as I still have to go. Does that make sense?"

"It makes sense in a crazy sort of way," she said. "But do you really think you can live alone?"

"Why not? Living with my father is like living on my own. I know what needs to be done." I paused. "He's equipped me with what I need to go on. I know what to do."

All the times he'd woken me up, all the times he'd disappeared, the food in the basement, the money hidden around the house, the bank account, my having paid bills and shopped for groceries and fixed meals. All the time thinking he was going to die or leave me—all of it had prepared me. I could survive because I'd already survived so much.

"And then if people did find out I was living on my own in the house, I'd just take off and come here. I'd live in the forest. This is my *backup* backup plan."

Harmony got out of her chair and walked over to me. "You realize that this is sort of…sort of…"

"Desperate?" I asked.

"I was going to say crazy."

"I figured if anybody could understand it, you would."

She didn't answer.

"Maybe it doesn't all make sense…but it's all I have," I said.

"And I shouldn't take that away from you. Look, Robert, if anybody can make this work, it's you."

"I can make it work because I have no choice."

"And this is what you've been spending all your money on?" she said. "On camping stuff?"

"I've been putting some away too. I have almost a thousand dollars saved up."

"And here I was, wondering if you had enough money for a pair of pants," she said.

"I have enough to do what I have to do. Look, I better break down my camping stuff and pack it up before it gets dark."

"I can help," she offered.

"It's okay. I know exactly how it's all supposed to be packed away," I said.

"Still, isn't it good to have somebody here to help?"

I had to admit that it was. And it was even better to have finally shared my last secret with her.

# TWENTY

Our history teacher, Mrs. Green, had asked Harmony to go out into the hall with her to continue their "discussion" in private. They may have been out of sight, but they weren't out of sound and were really not private at all. Mrs. Greene had told everybody to continue silent reading, but nobody was reading. They were all listening in.

Raj leaned over. "You should go out there."

"What?"

"You might be able to stop it."

"He's right—you should go out there," Taylor said.

"I'm not that brave."

Raj and Taylor both chuckled.

The voices in the hall had gotten quieter, so maybe there was no need. Then they got louder again. At least, Harmony's did. I couldn't make out the words, but the anger was unmistakable. Then Mrs. Greene's voice came across loud and clear, followed by a burst from Harmony and then... silence.

The door opened and Mrs. Greene stepped back in. Harmony wasn't with her. Mrs. Greene closed the door behind her. Either Harmony had taken off or been sent to the office. One was bad and the other was worse.

I shot my hand into the air and didn't wait for Mrs. Greene to respond. "Can I go to the washroom?"

She nodded. I jumped up and headed for the door. Mrs. Greene was still there, and she leaned over and whispered in my ear, "I've sent her to the office...I didn't have any choice...try to calm her down if you can."

"Yes, ma'am."

I ran toward the office. I hoped I could get to Harmony before she reached it. If she kept escalating, it wouldn't just be getting kicked out of class. She could get suspended and kicked out of school for the rest of the day or even longer.

The office had come into sight, but Harmony hadn't. I peeked through the glass. She wasn't there. Mrs. Henry waved, and I waved back.

I had to think. Where would Harmony have gone instead? There was her locker, the isolated hall at the back of the auditorium where we sat sometimes, or maybe she'd just gone, walked out. I'd try the last possibility first and work my way back through the other two.

I ran along the hall and out the back door. I went into the yard just in time to see her make the turn toward the street. I ran across the yard and caught up to her. She didn't look surprised to see me.

"You can't just walk away."

"Watch me." She started walking again, and I ran and put myself in front of her.

"Look, just go to the office, say you're sorry, and that's the end of it."

"I'm not sorry. Do you want me to lie?" she asked.

"Of course I do. Look, you'll get suspended if you just take off."

"How stupid. If I leave school, they won't let me go to school?"

"I didn't say it was smart. Please. You've been doing so well. You've gone six weeks without a suspension. Isn't that, like, your record?"

"Close."

Her expression had softened ever so slightly.

"Come on. If you get suspended, you'll prob-ably get grounded, and if you get grounded you can't go shopping with me after the basketball game like you promised. Do you want to be respon-sible for what I buy without you?"

She smiled, and then she laughed. "Just so I understand, you're arguing that your lack of taste is the reason I should come back?"

"Basically. That and because I'm asking you to. Please?"

"How can I say no to a boy who counts down days and thinks camping by the railroad tracks is an answer to a long-term place to live?"

"I'm hoping you can't. Come on."

I took her by the hand and started walking back to the school. She didn't fight me. "What's your magic number?" she asked.

"Fifteen hundred and eighty-four days. Yours?" I asked.

"Twenty-three days until she's through rehab."

"And how long after that before you think she might be ready to take you back?" I asked.

"It could be another month or longer, depending on when she can find a place to live and apply to the agency to get me back."

"She's still going to be looking for a place around here, right?"

"That's the plan."

"Everybody needs a plan," I said.

"And at least two backup plans, I've been told."

Harmony—and her social worker—had convinced her mother that it was important for Harmony to have "continuity" and that it would help her mother's case to have her return to her care if she found a place around here when she got out of rehab. They were looking for an apartment that was close enough for Harmony to finish out the year at Osler. I wanted that. But what I *really* wanted was for her to live with the Watsons and walk to and from school with me every day. That wasn't just me being selfish. Why would Harmony returning to her mother be any better this time than all the other times?

"Basically, your magic number is twenty-three plus the thirty days to find a place, for a total of fifty-three. That's not long," I said.

"That's assuming she makes it through the program."

"She's gone this far, so why wouldn't she finish?"

Harmony didn't answer. I knew they had a telephone call every second day and were supposed to have spoken the night before and…

Her having problems today made sense now. "Yesterday's call didn't go so well, did it?" I asked.

"Not the best. She was complaining that she really didn't need treatment any longer, that staying was a waste of her time." Harmony let out a big sigh.

"She's still there. We'll talk while we're shopping. Don't worry, your detention won't be that long," I said.

She skidded to a stop. "I'm going to get a detention?"

"Oh yeah, you're definitely getting a detention for being tossed out of class, but isn't a twenty-minute detention before the game a lot better than a one-day suspension?"

"Fine."

She started walking. I trailed after her along the hall and right up to where she headed into the office. I waited just off to the side so I could see through the glass that she was talking to the secretary. Then, as she sat down on the bench, I headed back to class.

# TWENTY-ONE

I came in the front door and Candy greeted me as usual. I had worked hard, but Mrs. Priamo had fixed me a great meal before I started work. I liked the Priamos a lot. They were always nice to me. Lots of people were nice to me. Teachers, neighbors. My friends and Harmony. I didn't include her in the friends category because she was more than just a friend. She was my best friend. I figured even Sal knew that now.

My father was home. He didn't respond when I said hello. He just sat there, staring at the TV. The elevator was almost all the way down. I could see it in his expression and in the way he sat on the couch. He was still functioning, but he was headed to a place where he wouldn't be.

He excused himself—said how "tired" he was and went to bed. I'd make a point of setting my alarm extra early to make sure he got up in the morning. I'd make him some breakfast and pack a lunch for him and see that he got off to work.

★

I watched him drive away. He'd been in a reasonable mood this morning. I was positive he'd slept through the night, and sleep could make things better.

I just wished I could have slept as well as him. I'd lain awake going through all my plans and backup plans. Eventually I'd drifted off about two in the morning. I'd even gotten up and done some counting. I'd opened my notebook and since it was after midnight, I had changed the number to 1,580. That was a nice round number. Day by day it was working.

The phone rang, and I ran to answer it. I knew who it would be. Nobody else would be calling me at seven in the morning.

"Hey, Harmony, how are you—"

"It's not Harmony, Robert. It's Darlene—Mrs. Watson."

"Um...hello...how are you?" There could only be bad reasons she was calling me.

"I'm sorry to call you this early."

"Is something wrong?"

"Harmony ran away last night."

My heart rose up into my throat.

"My husband and I have been up most of the night."

"When did she leave?" I asked.

"Sometime after we went to bed. We didn't discover she was gone until about one in the morning when I heard a noise. It must have been the back door closing when she left."

"And you don't have any idea where she is?"

"I was hoping you'd know," she said.

"I don't know anything."

"We're all pretty worried...scared."

I was both.

"But why would she run? Things were going so well." Wait. "Did her mother take off from rehab again?"

"Yes, she left the treatment center."

"Then Harmony's probably gone to the East End to look for her."

In my mind I quickly ran through the bars we'd gone to. I remembered the name of the bar where we'd met Jeff. Should I tell Mrs. Watson that's where she might be? If I did, I would have to explain that we'd been there before.

"We know where her mother is." There was a pause. "I'm really not supposed to tell. It's all very confidential, but you deserve to know. Harmony's mother has been arrested."

"Arrested for what?" I exclaimed.

"She was caught with drugs and then she resisted arrest. It sounds serious. The social worker told Harmony and me that it could be half a year before it even goes to court, and then Valerie could be facing at least six months in jail, maybe more, if she's convicted."

A year. Harmony couldn't go home to her mother for at least a year. That was why she'd run.

"We told her that she could stay here for as long as she needs to," Mrs. Watson said.

I knew she would have said that to reassure Harmony, but it would have done the opposite.

"Robert, you'd tell me if you knew where she was, wouldn't you?"

"Of course! You know, she told me you're the best people she's ever been with."

Mrs. Watson let out a big sigh. "That makes me feel at least a bit better. I was thinking that somehow it was our fault."

"It wasn't." I wanted to tell her about Harmony saying they were so nice that their home would be a good place for me to go, but I couldn't without telling her too much.

"If you hear, if she calls, you'll let us know… right?"

"Yeah, of course. And if she calls, I'll try to get her to come back."

"Thank you, Robert. If there's one person in the world she'll listen to, I think it's you."

It was nice of Mrs. Watson to say that, but if Harmony really listened to me, she wouldn't have run in the first place.

We said goodbye and I put the phone down. What now? Could I just go to school and try to pretend that Harmony wasn't missing? Should I go and look for her? No, that made no sense—I didn't know where to even start. Maybe she would show up at school or be there somewhere along the way, waiting for me. There was only one way to find out.

*

I gave Candy the last little corner of my toast. She gobbled it up. She had been all over me this morning. She knew I was anxious. I thought about how Candy needed me, how she was one of the reasons I'd never run away or go away. I needed her too.

I'd worked hard to follow routine this morning. Routine stopped me from thinking, stopped me from feeling, stopped me from worrying.

Okay, that was a lie. Nothing stopped those things completely, but routine helped.

My father always accused me of worrying too much. I thought I was doing well not to worry *all* of the time.

If Harmony was planning to meet me along the way, I had to follow the routine we always followed. I'd packed a second sandwich—peanut butter—for Harmony. She would have missed breakfast and would be hungry. Then I could try to convince her to go back to the foster home— although I was worried that she'd try to convince me to run away with her. I wasn't running anywhere. Even if her plan had fallen apart, I still had my mine, and I had to stick with them.

I said goodbye to Candy, squeezed out the door, clicked the lock and pulled the door closed. I was partway down the walk when I turned. I had to go back and check. Unavoidable. Two steps up, one big bounce across the porch. The door was locked. Time to go to school, and hopefully Harmony would be there or somewhere along the way, waiting for me....

And then I thought of where she might be instead.

I went around the side of the house and to the shed. I pulled open the door. My pack was gone.

* ⭐ *

Coming up to the railroad tracks, I saw that one of the clips for holding the mesh to the fence was on the ground. I picked it up as I looked around to see if I was being watched. There was nobody. I took off the second clip, peeled away the mesh and stepped through the opening. As quickly as possible I sealed up the fence and then ran along the embankment. I retraced the steps I'd taken dozens of times. Approaching the forest, I hesitated for a second at the path that led into the clearing. I listened as I continued to walk. I could hear birds, some traffic in the distance, but nothing else. I stepped into the clearing. There was my tent, and there was Harmony, sitting in the camping chair. She gave me a little wave.

"I was wondering when you'd show up."

"How did you know I'd think to look here?" I asked.

"You're smart. I thought you might have even come last night."

"I didn't know you were missing until this morning when Mrs. Watson called. She wanted to know if I knew where you were."

"And what did you tell her?"

"I told her I didn't know."

"Thanks for not telling."

"When she called, I *didn't* know. It wasn't until I started walking to school that it came to me, and I checked the shed."

"I didn't think you'd mind if I borrowed your stuff. Besides, it wasn't like I could knock on your door in the middle of the night and tell your father I wanted to borrow your camping stuff."

"Okay, probably better you didn't."

"If I had asked you, would you have said yes?" she asked.

I shrugged. "I would have tried to talk you into going home."

"I don't have a home."

"Your foster home. They're pretty worried about you."

"I don't care."

"I was worried too," I said.

"Sorry."

I sat down on the ground right beside her. I was waiting for her to say something, and I figured she was waiting for me to say something. I knew she was more stubborn than me, so I'd have to break the silence.

"What was it like sleeping here last night?"

"I didn't really get a lot of sleep. It was late when I left, later when I figured out to grab your stuff, and then setting up in the dark with just the lamp for light wasn't easy. And it's, well, a little spooky being out here."

"The first time was for me too. I started bringing Candy with me after that."

"I guess I should have borrowed your dog as well," she joked.

"Yeah, that would have helped. Look, I heard about your mother."

She didn't say anything.

"So what happens from here?" I asked.

"She's in jail until the trial and will probably be in jail after the trial."

"I meant about you. What happens to you?"

"This is what happens to me," she said.

"You're going to stay here, in this tent?

"Isn't that what you were going to do? Isn't this your plan?"

"First off, it's my backup backup plan, and we've both agreed it's not a great plan," I said. "Come on, you have to go to the Watsons.'"

"No I don't, and you can't make me."

"You're right. I can't make you, but you can't stop me from going there and telling them where you are," I said.

"If you do that, by the time you get back I'll have left, and it won't just be me that's gone. I'll take some of your camping stuff with me."

"I hope you won't do that," I said.

"Because you don't want to lose your precious stuff?"

"Because I don't want to lose *you*, you idiot!"

I think we both were surprised by what I'd said. Me, not that I wasn't thinking it but that I'd actually said it out loud.

"Besides, this camping stuff isn't even my backup backup plan anymore."

"It's not? Then what is?"

"You are," I said.

"Me?"

"You. I'm counting on you to help me when things get rough."

She chuckled. "I thought you were slightly crazy when this was your backup plan, but it isn't as crazy as relying on me."

"No, I do rely on you."

"Rely on me to screw up or run away or punch you in the face or say the wrong thing. Those things you can rely on me for."

"You're wrong," I said, trying to sound as convincing as I could.

"How am I wrong?"

"You just are—" I stopped.

"Well, go ahead and tell me how."

"Not today."

"What?" she demanded.

"Tomorrow. I'll explain it, but not until tomorrow."

"That is so pathetic. Do you think you can get me to go back by offering some stupid lie?" she asked.

"It's not stupid and it isn't a lie. It's a promise." I paused. "Look, if I can't give you a reason, a really good reason, to stay, then you can run away the day after that."

She didn't look completely convinced, but she was softening.

"Okay, I'll give you twenty-four hours to convince me to stay," she said.

"And if I can give you a good reason, you have to promise not to run. Not tomorrow or the next day or the week after that. You'll stay put, right?"

"Okay, but you need to explain one more thing to me."

"Okay, I'll try," I said

"What makes you think you can get out of here when everything says you can't make it?"

I shook my head. "I don't know. I just know I can."

"That's not good enough. If you can explain to me why you're so positive you can make it, then maybe I can make it too."

"I just don't know."

"Then you better start thinking about it. You can start when you're walking me back to the foster home."

Harmony got up. She bent over, picked up the camping chair and started to fold it up.

"Do you think you could come inside with me when we get there to talk to Mrs. Watson?" she asked.

"If you want me to be there, then I'm there."

"She'll probably call the social worker or even the police, and they might all come over," Harmony said.

"I'll be there when you talk to all of them, if that's what you want."

"That's what I want."

I started to fold up the tent and she started to put things in the backpack.

"Robert, do you know the real reason you can't be my boyfriend?"

"Because I'm funny, I remind you of your grandmother, most relationships don't work, and you can't afford to lose me. Does that just about cover it?" I asked without stopping my task.

"There's one more. You can do better than me."

I put the tent in the pack and looked at her. "Don't put yourself down."

"I'm not. You deserve somebody who'll treat you right, who'll be a good wife and a good mother to your kids someday. Somebody who doesn't have a bad temper and who went to university... that's probably where you'll meet her."

"Stop talking like that."

"And her family will be really normal—she'll have two parents, and they'll really love each other."

"Just stop."

"She'll be somebody who's completely different from my mother and—"

"Stop now!" I yelled at the top of my lungs.

To my surprise she did.

"For now, let's just make sure we don't lose the one friend who actually understands the other. Okay?"

She nodded.

"Good," I said. "And just for your information, I don't have to be the only one in this neighborhood who makes it out." I paused. "There could be two."

~~1,580~~ 1,519

# TWENTY-TWO

I stood just inside the Watsons' front door as Mrs. Watson talked with Harmony. At least this morning I could be off to the side. The previous day, when I'd brought her home, I'd had to talk to her foster parents, the social worker and the police. We'd told them all that I'd run into her on the way to school. I hadn't thought any of them believed me at first. We hadn't told them anything about where we had talked or my camping stuff or where she'd spent the night.

Mrs. Watson was telling Harmony a lot of the same things she'd said the day before—that she cared for her, that they wanted her to stay, that everybody makes mistakes. Harmony was grounded for the rest of the week and the weekend coming up, but Mrs. Watson wanted her to know they were doing this because they cared for her. Harmony wasn't talking much, but she wasn't arguing at all.

Anxiously I looked at my watch. I didn't want to be late today. Harmony's social worker and foster mother had called the school the day before to explain what had happened, why I'd been away all morning. When I'd shown up in the afternoon, Mr. Yeoman had told me he was proud of me, and Mr. Arseneau had called me down to the office and said he always expected me to do the right thing—that I was a leader, and he knew I'd go far in life. It felt good to have people believe in me.

The bad part was that they'd had to call my father at work to let him know what had happened. I'd thought he might mention it to me when he got home—tell me I'd done something good or that I shouldn't have done it or something—but he didn't. I hadn't been surprised, but I was still disappointed. Somehow even expecting to be disappointed didn't completely stop the disappointment when it happened.

Harmony and her foster mom came into the hall. "Sorry to keep you waiting," Mrs. Watson said.

"That's okay. We have time."

"Thank you for walking with her to school. And thank you again for bringing Harmony back to us yesterday."

"I just walked her here. It was her decision."

Mrs. Watson reached out and gave Harmony a big hug. To my surprise, Harmony hugged her back.

Then Mrs. Watson hugged me. At first my arms just hung at my sides, and then I brought up my right arm and placed it around her.

"You two better get going."

We did. We didn't just have to walk to school. Harmony and I had to have time to talk.

I grabbed my pack off the floor and slung it over one shoulder. We were off. This could be like every other school day for the past two months.

"I packed a jam sandwich and a peanut-butter sandwich," I said.

"You're pretty confident."

"Don't we always trade lunches?"

"Confident that I'm going to be there for lunch. Twenty-four hours is almost up. You have the rest of the walk to convince me not to take off."

"Didn't you just promise Mrs. Watson that you'd go to school?"

"You promised me you'd give me a reason to stick around. Are you going to keep your promise?"

I reached into my pocket. "I have something for you. Hold out your hand."

She did, and I pulled it out and placed it in her palm.

"You're giving me a piece of broken crayon?" she asked.

"I've giving you back the piece you gave me on the streetcar."

"You kept it?"

"You gave it to me."

"And you said it was stupid."

"It sounded stupid, but it wasn't. There are lots of broken crayons out there."

"All I see are broken crayons," Harmony said.

"Or crayons that are worn down from being used too long or too hard or because a new package of crayons is too expensive or—"

"Could you stop with the crayons?"

I shrugged. "You and I know we're broken. Most people don't see that in themselves or don't find out until it's too late, or they're too old, or they've already made so many bad decisions that there's no way back. If you're broken and you know it, you have to get up every day and work harder and longer than everybody else if you want to get anywhere."

"Which is what you do."

"What *you* need to do too. And even then, doing all of that, there's no guarantee of success."

"Then why bother if you're just going to lose anyway?"

"Because there's a chance. And if you don't try, there's no chance," I said.

"Don't you ever want to just give up?"

I laughed. "Sometimes I don't even want to get out of bed in the morning. I want to run away or disappear or quit."

"But you don't."

I nodded. "But I don't."

"We could run away together," said Harmony.

"I'm not running away from anything. I'm not giving up."

"Why? Why don't you give up, and why shouldn't I give up?"

"If I tell you, you'll think I'm stupid."

"I think lots of things about you, but stupid isn't one of them. Tell me. I need to know why I should even try," Harmony said.

I let out a deep sigh. "You know my mother died before I was old enough to start school."

"I know. You were four."

"My grandmother walked me to and from school on my first day. I was so happy to see her waiting for me. I ran up to her, and she gave me a hug and told me how proud my mother would have been of me for going to school."

I took another deep breath. This wasn't easy. It wasn't something I'd ever told anybody or even said out loud to myself.

"I remember how that felt, thinking that my mother was proud of me. I guess I still want to make her proud of me."

"How do you make a dead person proud of you?" Harmony asked.

"Well, I just know she knows."

"Do you think she's sitting on some cloud somewhere, staring down at you?"

"I don't know. I just know I still want to make her proud."

"There's nothing I could ever do to make my mother proud," she said. I could hear a catch in her voice.

"Then don't do it for your mother—unless it's maybe to prove her wrong. Do it to make your grandmother proud. Maybe she's sitting on the same cloud as my mother, and they're both watching us and talking."

"I don't believe in God or Heaven."

"I'm just asking you to believe in your grandmother and try to make her proud of you."

"She used to tell me she was proud of me all the time."

"That must have felt really good."

She nodded ever so slightly and started to cry. She brushed away the tears as if she was trying to hide them from me.

"Then do good things that would make her proud and imagine telling her. That's what I do with my mother."

Her whole body shuddered, and she started sobbing louder. I reached out and wrapped one arm around her, then a second.

"I have one more thing for you."

"Is it the rest of the crayon?" she said and chuckled through the tears.

"It's a letter for you. From me."

"Why are you giving me a letter?"

"I want you to be able to read what I just said. Over and over again, whenever things get tough, whenever you feel like quitting." I pulled it out of my pocket and handed it to her.

It was folded, and she straightened it out. On the front was her name.

"You wrote my name in crayon."

"I wrote the whole letter in crayon…with the broken crayon you gave me that I just gave back to you."

"But why?"

"You have to always remember this. Broken crayons still color."

"Do you really believe that?" she asked.

"I wouldn't have said it if I didn't."

"Talk is cheap. You want me to do the right thing. How about if you do the right thing too?"

"I do. Every day."

"No, you don't. You're just hanging in there. Do you really think you can keep on living the way you're living?"

"I've done it this long," I said.

"You've done it too long. And when it does break down with your father, do you think you're going to live on your own or sleep in a tent by the railroad tracks?"

"I'll do what I need to do."

"What's the count?" she asked.

"Fifteen hundred and seventy-nine days."

"That's a long time."

"Not as long as it was when you first showed up, and tomorrow it will be one day less. I'll survive."

"I know you will, but don't you ever think you deserve better than just surviving?" she asked.

"It's better than not surviving."

"You should have more than that. You're a smart guy. You're going to figure out something better." She paused. "Tell you what. I'll stick around until you do."

"That could take a long time."

"The most it could take is 1,579 days." She paused. "Who knows? I might have to get my own notebook and do my own countdown."

# TWENTY-THREE

It had been a good month. No, it had been a *great* month. Harmony had kept her word. She was happier, doing better in school, and it seemed like the Watsons had become her backup plan. And for me, in some ways, Harmony had become my backup plan.

My father had been doing better too. So much better that I'd started to believe it was all going to be okay and that I wouldn't need backup plans.

But now here it was, two in the morning, and he hadn't come home and he hadn't called. I hadn't seen this one coming. I'd thought everything was going so well. How could I have been so stupid? Higher hopes had just led to a bigger fall.

Candy started to whine, and I reached down and gave her a scratch. I wanted to tell her it was going to be all right, but I didn't like to lie to her. I kept staring out the front window.

Over the past hour the street had gone from quiet to completely deserted. There were no cars, nobody out walking their dogs. It was dark except for the streetlights. Only one house, halfway up the block and on the other side, still had lights on. I'd turned off our lights so that if someone were to walk by, they wouldn't see me staring out the window.

Even if my father didn't come home tonight, I could survive. I'd done it before and I could do it again…and again…and again. Earlier in the evening I'd thought about calling Harmony, but now it was too late. Besides, she'd have given me a hard time about the situation and demanded to know what I was going to do.

I knew he wouldn't be coming home, so why was I standing in the window, watching and waiting? I knew I should go to bed and try to get to sleep. There was really nothing else I could do. I'd wake up in the morning and another day would be gone,

one more ticked off the count. I'd lasted this long, so what was another 1,548 days? My whole body shuddered. Fifteen hundred and forty-eight more days and nights. *Could* I survive? Maybe Harmony wasn't the only who deserved better. There was just one way to find out.

I walked across the room and stopped in front of the phone. I reached to pick it up but drew back my hand like it was too hot to handle.

I forced myself to pick it up and punched in the numbers. I knew the number by heart. It started to ring. *Maybe I should just hang up before they answer.*

"Hello?"

I paused for a few seconds. There was no going back once I spoke. "Hello, Uncle Jack. It's Robbie."

"Robbie! Are you all right?"

"I'm sorry for bothering you, especially this late."

"Robbie, whatever it is, I'm glad you called. Can you hold on a second? I want your aunt to come on the line as well."

I heard him yell out, "Cora, take the other phone! It's Robbie!"

I heard her voice in the background. "Robbie! Why would he be calling at this time—is he all right?"

Within a few seconds the second line clicked. "Robbie, is something wrong?" my aunt asked.

"Yes…yes…I need help."

"Is it your father?" my uncle asked.

"He's not here—he hasn't come home."

"Has he been in an accident? Has something happened?"

I shook my head, then realized they couldn't see me. "No, he does this."

"Does what?"

I took a deep breath. I'd come too far to turn back. "He takes off, sometimes for days at a time."

"And leaves you alone?" Aunt Cora asked.

"Yes."

"That's…that's…well…he can't do that to you," she said.

"We're coming to get you," Uncle Jack said.

"We'll be there in a few minutes," Aunt Cora said. "You're staying here with us tonight."

"I can't leave Candy."

"Your dog is as welcome here as you are—you know that."

I didn't. I didn't know anything. I had only hoped.

"But it could be days. He was once gone almost a week," I said.

My uncle swore. I'd never heard him swear before.

"You're welcome here as long as you need," my aunt said.

"You're welcome here forever," my uncle said. "Forever."

I started to cry. I couldn't help myself.

"It's going to be all right," my aunt said. "You know how much we love you."

Maybe I should have known, but I hadn't. Not until now.

"Get your things together. We'll see you soon."

"Thank you."

I put the phone down.

I looked at Candy, who was staring up at me. She looked worried.

"It's going to be okay, girl," I said. And maybe for the first time ever, I actually believed it.

# POST NOTE

This is the end of the novel, but it isn't the end of the story. I want you to know what happened.

Except for one short period when she went back to live with her mother, Harmony managed to hang in at the Watsons' until she completed high school. She went on to college, where she majored in drama. Robbie always kids her that she's been a drama major since the first day he met her. She dropped out in the middle of her second year of college when she was offered a part in a movie— her big break. She became pretty successful, and you probably know her. She doesn't go by the name Harmony though. She took a stage name—hint: it's the name of a state.

She never married, but she adopted two children. She is a great mother. She secretly donates large sums of money to donkey sanctuaries across North America because she wasn't so much a broken crayon as she was a stubborn donkey. Despite her schedule, travels and fame, she and Robbie stay in contact. He's still the only person she trusts completely.

Robbie stayed with his aunt and uncle for 1,548 days—although, after the first few hundred days, he stopped marking off the days in his notebook. He didn't need to count them anymore. After he finished high school, he went to university and graduated. He found the woman of his dreams, and they got married. They had wonderful children. He built the family he never had and cherishes them every day. They remain the center of his world. He still spends his life working harder every day than anybody else. He still checks each locked door a second time, and sometimes in the middle of the night he reaches for his wife's hand, then goes back to sleep, happy and content, because, really, broken crayons still color. And those colors can be so beautiful.

# NOTE FOR EDUCATORS

I grew up in poverty. It's not an affliction or a disease that needs to be cured. But it is a culture as distinct as other cultures. It comes with traditions, myths and rituals. Being poor means growing up at a severe disadvantage. Life is tougher, harder, more difficult and, at times, seemingly impossible. You discover that life isn't fair and that the deck is stacked against you. You grow up believing you're not as good as other people, not as good as you need to be. And even if you can somehow fool other people, you never really and truly convince yourself.

Some people get out. Somehow. I got out. You learn that you have to work harder than everybody else. If you're lucky, you find people along the way—usually, in the beginning, it's a teacher or two or three—who see you and what you are capable of doing.

The hard part for teachers isn't discovering the potential inside these young people but rather in convincing them that they really do have that potential. Potential for success, for great things, to become so much more. To be loved and valued. You have to convince them and show them that, despite their realities, success is possible. And when they try to prove you wrong by saying or doing something to sabotage their journey, you need to say it louder. Tell them you believe in them, that they deserve to succeed. And then tell them again. And again and again and again. And then again. And again. If the whole world keeps telling them they can't win, you're going to have to tell them more often and yell louder that they can succeed.

Why should those positive words from teachers mean more than what these young people see around them? Because words are powerful. Words can change the world—at least, the world of that student. You can be the person who changes lives— it's probably why you became a teacher to begin with. I know you won't let them down.

— *EW*

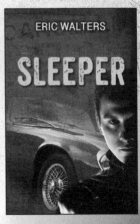

*Eric Walters* is the award-winning author of more than 100 novels and picture books. He is a tireless presenter, speaking to over 100,000 students per year in schools across the country. A Member of the Order of Canada, Eric lives in Guelph, Ontario.